Pasty
Pale
DARKNESS

The sides of presentation that intersect yet repel away by
the core of a melted molten hybrid that contradicts and confuses
the applied science of history . Believe not what you see or hear.
The truth is still a figment of a lie. Enter the daunting views of
a split personality disorder whose scruples change with the wind.

 For information address: Michael Wade Johnson
At www.facebook.com/Micwj
Email at: Micwjohnson@aol.com

DESIGNED by Mic Wade Johnson
Cover created by James C. Coffelt other_studios@hotmail.com

Writing for reading for relating

BIO : Michael Wade Johnson was born in Tompkinsville, KY in 1976
And grew up near Hermitage Springs, TN or so his thoughts tell him
But could they be wrong? Absolutely.

Pasty Pale Darkness – the heads and tails of it all

Book 5 for those of you keeping score

writings : yeah , tasteful : well…

Also available from writer Michael Wade Johnson :
Poet's Journal, Misery Melodies & Dirty Dirges, Defining Love, and **Nymph's Denial**

Enter book 5: Pasty Pale Darkness. A cumulative collection of words I put down starting around August 2002. I've worn these topics pretty thin so bear with me while I endeavor once more into my own personal lunacy.

Why "Pasty Pale Darkness" you ask? Well, I chose the title for various reasons. Mainly the overall theme addressed in these pages reflects stories of hypocrisies and the way too apparent duality of man. Ah, the irony we embrace. The jekyll/hyde if you will. Another motive for the title was the fact that I am a very pale skinned individual yet inside I feel dark and forebodingly luminous. This all adds to the contradictions that reside within these pages.

This book is divided into 3 sections. The pasty pale side, the side that shines light on my normally abnormal thoughts, is the beginning chapter. Typical Mic stories can be found here. The darkness side, however, is a view that burrows deep into my chaotic horror infested imagination and stirs up the demons that sleep within. This division also includes six short stories known as the dark scripts. The lyrics part contains songs that I wrote for my band during the course of shaping this book.

With this book I stopped giving titles to each individual piece of work because I grew tired of creating one and then months or years later, seeing the title popularized by another artist in the creative field. Thus I decided to allow the words to go title less and just be numbered, signifying my need to not follow the masses. Such a rebel. Ha.

Most of the book was written in late 2002 and 2003. Some in 2004. Short stories written late 2004 and 2005.

Pasty Pale
Side
Pages #7-57

Darkness
Side
Pages #58-111

Lyrics
Side
Pages #112-138

Pasty Pale

Side

the side that shines light on those normally abnormal thoughts

001

this window holds
oily nose smudges
from lonely longing faces
staring for salvation
across the horizon
a long awaited answer
a fulfillment for you
take that unexpected chance
leap into upliftment
i can't jump for you
you have to face your fear alone
do it soon
before the smearing smothers
and you can't see out
the proverbial window.

002

this map is too hard to read
the direction's irrelevant anyway
i never know where I'm going
the map couldn't possibly help
i never know where I'm at
i can't navigate myself
take the wheel anyone
drive me to my destination
pave the way for me
cause I'm lost again
every place looks the same
every curve leads to nowhere
i never know where I'm going
maybe I'm just pushing the pedals
running the treadmills
i never know where to turn
or who to turn to
the map is useless to me
i'm feeling in the darkness
driving without lights at night
everyone looks the same
but no one appears familiar
highways turn into headaches
the map is blurring
and nothing seems real
my breakdown halts progress
repairs needed too often
i never know where I'm going
i'm forever lost in limbo
shove this in park…

003

welcome to the geekshow
eyeliner for everyone
maybe just a pair of slacks
and some octagon glasses
after awhile every rock n roll fan
bears similar traits and styles
individualist becomes fashionable norm
and nothing is sacred
everything is borrowed and blue
i don't want to be you
no, not the clone of you
accents and anecdotes
blend into one meshed mumble
as predictable as they come
show that metal sign
let me see that lighter
i can't do this dance anymore
let me evolve.

004

you can't talk to someone
without fucking them
you can't have any friends
or any personal privacy
no escape from the rumors
people have to entertain themselves
with true or false trivialities
slandering others to make themselves
forget about their own jaded past
not from saints lips do these lies come
but from the mouths of hypocrites
who cannot find a real hobby
pry open my insides and view
giggle at every little abnormality
and ignore the shortcomings
that the mirror will not hide.

005

go ahead bring up the weather
go ahead try and be clever
go ahead state the obvious
go ahead be certain and boisterous
go ahead quoting your nonsense
go ahead I'll finish your sentence
go ahead smile that fake smile
go ahead tell me your profile
go head show me the typical
go ahead no need to be topical
go head laugh at your own jokes
go ahead choke on your quick tokes
go ahead impress all with your skill
go head marvel everyone at will
go ahead tell me the same one again
go ahead my interest I'll pretend
go ahead with that usual routine
go ahead while I just want to scream…

006

misjudged
I misjudged you
maybe I wanted to
you weren't being you
someone I never really knew
that's the real you
you cannot be
the person whom I see
looking back at me
misjudged terribly
in the distance
sheer magnificence
up close and near
not as you appeared
a shadow puppet
formed from dirty hands
I misjudged my place
I can never be your man

007

bring me up to speed
I'm too slow to comprehend
this culture and I collide
nothing do I understand
what makes you tick?
volunteer and I'll dissect
observe each movement
so easy to predict
values and rules
only fools follow
prod me and I fight
won't sit, eat, and swallow
the opinion of another
slip me another suggestion
rolling my eyes I laugh
gracefully declining the mission
my time is <u>my</u> time…

008

we had spoken to each other a few times
then our first night together
pick you up at your house, met the family
awkward silences and nervous fumbling hands
we drove around all the nearby towns
talked about life, ups and the downs
for a moment we seemed perfectly compatible
through all the courteousness and withholds
isn't that how the story always goes?
we both knew the attraction was heavy
yet for awhile we pretended to be civilized
then we stopped and parked at the Dairy Burger
gradually our heads gravitated together
and in that spot we had our first kiss
more like mouth-to-mouth intercourse
taking turns slurping saliva and tongue
we resumed driving while never stopping exchange
for the next hour or two the night was ours
you straddled me as I tried to navigate
making out on country roads and city limit streets
couldn't see the road for your frame in my face
you mauled me with your fiery kisses
groping and rubbing as I tried to steer
as we drove the real drive was happening inside
never got caught frenching in the front seat
and somehow we safely survived
drove you back home with tasseled hair
blood red cheeks and clawed collarbone
and we agreed to do it again sometime
now all I have are a couple of photographs
to remind me of a girl who knew no rules
a girl who took the passenger privilege seriously
teenage hormones unstoppable and uncontainable
so she unleashed them on me that night
we used it to our advantage
it took us farther than we ever imagined.

009

lose your dignity
shave your head for me
prove your self-worth
lose those brown curls
shave away attraction
prove you can take reaction
lose the vanity hold
prove you have enough soul
shave the sexy image
lose only superficialness
prove you're more than a look
shave it off, I'll still be hooked !

010

these lines aren't about girls
so they really aren't worth reading
put it down, toss it aside
not even worth the time to view
they're about mayonnaise and the Milky Way
about fire hydrants and fire ants
about philosophy jargon at a bargain
about icy snow storms and kittens warm
about soul searching and sweet gherkins
about theme park rides and show slides
about 7 wonders and deafening thunder
about comic books and comic looks
about hair fads and hair days bad
about nothing relating to the heart
about nothing but my eccentric art
girls won't be mentioned
not even metaphorically
no tale of discreet discretions
the plot wanes over insignificances
never touching the topic that matters
the only important issue ignored
what a waste of paper.

011

I wasn't breast-fed
I was fed only lies
Earned no people skills
Can't begin to try
Gloomy tadpole stages
Broken from the start
Missing that missing link
Missing a working heart
I wasn't taught right
Thrown into worlds of my own
Left to understand from scratch
Left to grow up all alone
Common everyday events
Throw me into upheaval
Sit solitary in a corner
Give the impression of evil
Merely needing to connect
Validate my meaning
Embrace this old soul
Devalue my demeaning
Let me drink the milk
Get me some structure
Too late to imitate
The lifestyle of another.

012

I'm not to good to…
Put elbows on the table
I'm not to good to…
Sit on your carpeted floor
I'm not to good to…
Walk around in boxers
I'm not to good to…
Have my heart broke some more
I'm not to good to…
Act like I'm a fool
I'm not to good to…
Disregard any rule of class
I'm not to good to…
Turn bad from bad turns
I'm not to good to…
Tell you to kiss my ass.

013

I could never be the same person everyday
Ho-hum humdrum and all
That's why I change in the simplest ways
A big boost from a detail small
I could never hold the same beliefs of yesterday
Trials of errors offset my mind
Contradicting everything I've ever knew
Cocoon and envelop a new breed this time…

You pretend to be interested
But you don't have a care
Nod as if you're listening
But your mind is not there
Cater to their obsessions
While you don't have a clue
They know only your portrayal
While never knowing what's really you…

She's a bitch – is that what makes her
so loveable?
Would she be so appealing
if she were a sweetheart?
I doubt it.
She wouldn't get the time of day
She'd just shrivel up and rot away
People are drawn to
  the strangest shit.

She says to her lover
"do you have any idea
the options I have right now?
But here I am
With you
What does that tell you?"

014

so far away from my hell of a home
scenes come quick in odd avenues unknown
no more familiar strangers flaunt in my face
people minding their own business, could get used to this place
no ex-girlfriends around every corner I see
wearing their skimpy clothes, trying to get to me
no more parental figures ordering every move I make
no one counts and tallies every little mistake
so far away from the land I never thought I'd leave
away from the simple conservative beliefs I don't believe
no longer buried in the past, I'm letting go
starting new ground, far away from everything I know.

015

sure, masturbation is therapeutic
however even the greatest pleasure
can dull after years of use
spice it up a little for stimulation
different hand, different stroking pattern
once I tied a rope and yanked
until arousal of orgasm
whacking with condoms is fun also
if time is of total leisure
letting hot water from a spout
beat down on the dick's bottom side
the sensitive area
(this may work for women as well)
will eventually result in climax
gloves and oils of course
also standing and sitting positions
varying will break the boredom
try changing your fantasy
and let the cum fall where it may.

016

Dana's got a mess
Got a dirty little secret
Dana's bag of bones
Got a closet where she keeps it
She stays in denial
Doesn't want to be on trial
For her new age style
That's been around for quite awhile
Girl on girl on girl
Not in this straight world
Girl on girl on guy
Seen not with this public eye
Girl on guy on guy
Sounds like a pornographic lie
If you want to succeed
The right way you better breed
At least pretend you do
Or they'll ostracize you too
Dana's got a heart
Got a head crammed full of goals
Dana's guilty pleasure
Preferring holes over poles
She stays in denial
Doesn't want to be on trial
For her new age style
That's been around for quite awhile
…
What a world
What a lie
When you have to hide
How you feel inside

Dana's got a date
On the other side of town
Strange and happy she is
So she can't be seen around
…

017

I've got to wean myself from you
Got to break this tie into
Now you're seeing him, some guy
And I can't look you in the eye
Never were you really mine
But I didn't feel so left behind
As these tears well up and fall
I realize I have lost it all
The thought of you with another
Chokes my hope as now I smother
Freezes my insides cold and hard
Nothing in life should be this hard
One more day, just one more chance
We could've began a great romance
Now as these tears well up and fall
I realize that I have lost it all
I have officially lost it all
At the time it seemed so small
You only conclude, in afterthought
Where you are and where you're not.

018

you're American
but it looks like you married
for a green card
looking at the two of you together
even the slightest spark
seems diminished by dullness
no passion, like a cover up disguise
perhaps you're secretly gay
and having a wife will ward off rednecks
and grants you the stealth shield
to do what you long to do: guys
maybc that's why I just see bullshit posing
becoming part of the census
maybe to get cheaper car insurance
but out of happiness – c'mon
I'm not fooled.

019

in the sweat stench of this concrete jungle,
nothing is as it appears
stay lowbrow and feed the vultures
fetish filled saints having ice cream
dreaming about being tied up in an abandoned shed by a rapist
the street is full of sweet illusion
whores pretending to be virgins
their bled and dried up hymens can be spotted 20 feet away
they'll deny it to the death
here there are no lines that people haven't crossed
the dealers have such outgoing flare
a personality to befriend any character
a grin as they're shoveling in
the dirt into the grave dug for users
users that were someone's ray of light
the light that never shines in this gothic setting
here I sit waiting for a bus to rescue me
take me back to my own personal rectangled room
where I'll tell myself that sleep will wash it all away
and tomorrow will be a better day in a more honest way.

020

saw your picture
didn't get your permission
suppose it doesn't matter now
saw you at your finest moment
captured on film by local pigs
leaving you available for wandering eyes
there you were, what were your thoughts?
wrapping that rope around durable limbs
did you pray? yell one last time?
curse the sky or leak a tear?
pre-planned or a coin toss?
the picture says it all
cold and isolated, haunting the hollowness
drool stringing down from your mouth
looked frozen midair, stopped in time
your pant leg displayed where urine oozed
the smell wouldn't have been pleasant as hours passed
what an embarrassment, what a way to go out
they also photographed your cum-stained sheets
and the pot remains in your ashtrays
as if these elements were as important
as you were there dangling in the wind.

021

How far will I go to solidify my desire for vengeance?
What resolution is reached when all morals are lost in the end?
Should I waste my time plotting destruction or rebuild my defenses?
Must I withhold from others and put up more invisible fences?
When will the damage done be outweighed by newfound hope?
Is there ever enough time to seal up the wound and begin to cope??

She cums like a man
Thick, white, and abundant
Spastic jerking seizures
She moans like she's dying
Maybe she is
Can't think of a better way
To go out with a bang
To savor the last breath
Sweet pain
Clinched in sweaty sex
Killed by passion
Perish by way of conception
Please let that be my death

Natacha Merritt, come to my town
For your spread, gladly I'd lay down
Digitize me, sexualize me
Tie me up and strap where you wish
I'll be your horny still-framed dish
Captivate me, fornicate me
We'll try every angle for artistic fun
Want to be a diary page of things already done
Want to be your entry as entry you permit
Want to be a memory as the photos you submit

022

Call me conceited, okay maybe I am
If such a hunky man, why's the gun in my hand?
Call me cocky, where does that come from?
An arrogant self-assured jerk, sorry I'm not one
Call me kinky, so I'm sadomasochistic
This dress I'm in just matches my lipstick
Call me complicated, complex to the bone
Try to decipher but you'll never crack this code
I'm prone to be alone
A laughing stock gnome
Ugly with bad tone
Singing lonesome songs
To the sky, my only home
To the one who'll never know.

023

trucks are to me
as crucifixes are to vampires
death is to life
as left side is to right side
ignorance is to humans
as carbon dioxide is to humans
self-destruction is to my brain
as hatred is to emotions
insanity is to reality
as serial killers are to their victims
guns are to murder
as satellites are to technology
blood is to my imagination
as lakes are to minnows
country music is to rock music
as weed whackers are to lawn mowers
my writing is to real writing
as Siamese midgets are to prom queens.

024

you made me mad
you pissed me off
now the games begin
let's see if the tables turn or not
with a word
with a look
reach into your heart
then twist it with my hook
look what I'm doing
to get under your skin
look how I'm playing
with your head so I can win
the upper hand, the tempo control
reversing all your thoughts and you never even know
we had a fight
an argument
now you're on your knees
but I won't forgive you yet
with a word
with a look
flirting with another
baby that was all it took
look what I'm doing
to get under your skin
look how I'm playing
with your head so I can win
the upper hand, the tempo control
reversing all your thoughts and you never even know

025

Can't believe I'm hearing this shit from you
Your moral values dictate self-leniency
You support no divine faith or spiritual judgment
Claim not to be a condemner of sins
Not Mr. Pious, more like the one least likely
If memory serves correctly, you have your stories
Your nights of sinful desires and betrayal
Is the past really that far behind?
Now you come with ridicule and belittlement for me
Try to make me feel guilty and undeserving
Have you found your salvation somewhere along the way?
And become a hypocrite to all your former ideals?
Because your words sound like religious propaganda
Have you wiped your slate clean, reformed yourself?
Have all your past discrepancies been forgiven?
Can you judge with a clear conscience now?
If not, then cut the holier than thou masquerade
You're not better than me
Remember that before you start your pathetic preaching.

026

he spent his days with hellish ways
never thought about an after phase
as years accumulated
the fear of death exasperated
he went to church after vowing never to go
with fingers crossed, he restored his soul
pretended to love an entity
posing only for the sympathy
to avoid any chance of condemnation
he settled for a sweet salvation
repented a cluster of disgusting deeds
as the moments of his time recedes
so he can be forgiven
and his essence can go on living
never before did he pray
now he's made that special change
his lips say he's a believer
but there're hints he's a deceiver.

027

don’t get too comfy, slut
you’re just a substitute lover
you only replace me when I can’t be there
don’t feel so fucking special, bitch
you’ll never be permanent
one day I’ll be the only one needed
and you’ll be history, cunt rag
you will be disposed of
and thrown away just like contraceptive.

Change my perspective
Look on the bright side for once
I try and I try
But I can’t keep from hating
Can’t <u>not</u> see the shit
Can’t ignore the intense damage
Tomorrow isn’t showing much promise
Can’t postpone the dread of existence
Sorry…I tried.

---

turn me down
you can’t turn me off
can’t silence my voice
it will be heard
one way or another.

028

trudging through the vast sewer of my over exhausted thoughts
there's this realm that appears again and again
in the center of my quaint vision stands a girl
a perfect specimen
one I never have to second-guess
one who demands nothing but gratitude
one who explores herself and her surroundings
one who gets the meaning without explanation
she is where my journey ends
I see hints of her everywhere
mix and match from girl to girl
but never the total combination
in one extravagant package
she is that hidden level
that secret passageway to the golden jewels
that link to happiness that otherwise that can't be found
she will change everything.

029

What do you say
When there's nothing to say?
What can I say
When I have nothing to say?
Silence drops hard like hail
When there's not a tale to tell
You ask me what I'm thinking
But there's not a scheme I'm making
I'm lost in the colors and rhythms
In my head where only I see them
We can connect without audible sounds
Come join me now, we'll fall to the ground
No words will be spoken aloud
But you'll hear me, I bet somehow
We'll converse in a different language
Then the need for talking we'll vanquish
What do you say
When there's nothing to say?
What do I say
When I have nothing to say?
Listen close, I'll find a way.

030

Sultry Sex Secret #5 :

We were on your parent's bed in the mid-afternoon
They were expected back any moment
That nervous fear stimulates the sexuality
After ripping each other's clothes off
And fondling every available body area
Together we were one
Making proper use of their queen-sized waterbed
Hot and sweaty, you were a luscious dream
We rolled and tumbled together in heated lust
You were panting and screaming for me to continue
I was grunting and moaning wildly, jerking feverishly
You thought it was out of fierce sexual pleasure
But actually a spasm shot through my leg
Tying that muscle into excruciating knots
I was in so much pain, I had to yell in agony
Oh well, we both got off just the same.

031

you said I had a small dick
when I was about average
you said I was short and stupid
when I was about average
those few little words
left an impact so substantial
sending this poor shmuck
into a pit of deep depression
fueled by self-loathing
and inadequacies
you didn't see the hours of torture
feeling so ugly and useless
your 2 minutes of comments
gave me 4 years of self-doubt
thank you for that.

You once were so freaky
Binds, blinds, and bondage
Handcuffs and leather everything
You wanted it here and there and everywhere
Now your conservative safe side
Is all I ever see
Now you've lost your taste for kinky
Or have you lost your taste for me?

Sacrifices never come without a bitter cost
And hearts and feelings are not regenerative
Once sliced open and drained of innocence
They never grow back the same again.

032

it was almost always cold
when we played
nights of being the rock star
surrounding the kerosene heater
trying to capture what little warmth
rose with the thick black smoke
that pushed out from the circular top
Zeke would play his solos and new riffs
thinking that it all went unappreciated
I would study the lyric sheet
trying to invoke the spirit of Kurt Cobain
the first few years we didn't have an agenda
we just played at random and had fun
there were parties and events we ignored
we skipped typical high school scenarios
instead we were creating sounds
thinking thoughts unimportant to peers
but we were located in the middle of nowhere
and no one understood
victims of the cultural disease
where potential gets compromised
as dreams get buried underneath the weight
of mediocrity and lack of availability
nevertheless, in that room
I felt more alive than ever before
like I was actually being productive
we didn't need girls, money, or politics
we survived on guitars, amps,
and words from the heart.

033

I'm a friend of a girl in love
We were closer friends
But she fell in love
Now she's one of those people
You know the type
When the personality splits
And out comes a jealous
And restrained creature
A person who has no time for you
Only time to be in love
A person whose thoughts cannot stray
From the power of her singular adoration
A girl in love, what a loss.

When I was 16
I was a novice
Who seemed to be
The first rugged pioneer
With raw emotions
Never felt by another human
My passions surpassed by far
Any that came before me

When you get to be my age
You see that everything
You have ever thought
Has came and went
Through the human cycle
Many times before you ever
Existed
Just another casualty to life.

034

I'm the spokesman for the simpletons
Hear me now as my voice calms your fears
And soothes the aches that occupy
The harrowing days of torrid work
With sweaty palms and dirty fingernails
Forget finding the reasons
Meanings aren't for the faint of heart
Leave that to the 2%
Leave it to the ones locked away
With charts and calculus diagrams
Leave it to me
I'll be the bearer of the burden
I'll reflect that oppression
Off your weary little head
And onto me where I'll soak up the spill
Complications made simple
And your eyes will see
Only the way they're taught
You speak the language you heard from birth
You also act from the actions set before you
Implanted subtly
You don't even taste it
Until it's too late
Don't worry about all that
I'll take care of the specifics
The details of mentality
Just go frolic in the sun
Have a happy time
As I turn more gray everyday
My fault, my ignorance
Consider yourself one of the lucky ones.

035

I'll be your case study
Your object of inanimate control
Push me away from my goals
Change my direction with new courses
Condition me with your methods
Customize me to your liking
Modulate me until I'm perfect
Test me everyday, every hour
Watch how I react to different stimulus
I'll learn the pattern of reinforcement
Become almost robotic
Then you will be happy
When everything I say you taught me
Every idea you implanted
Every action, every reflex – all from you
Brand me like cattle
Just a drone working for the queen
Just a slave for the master
All in the name of science
A statistical guinea pig
In the end, I'll be a picture for your files
And data for the textbooks
So let the fun begin…

036

company policy
rules based on a census of personal preference
how can you promote respect for individuality
and then dictate restrictions of garments
and personal ornaments?
no valid reason given
just means to push around the minority
an excuse of presentation for the masses
preventative to not offend the consumers
like they should control the appearance of a total stranger
how is this dress code not prejudice?
to consider a certain look or style flamboyant and distasteful
those stereotypes should be outdated
freedom of self-expression should exist
in a supposed free country
but instead we own the rights granted by the popular opinion
not necessarily the popular opinion of all residents
but rather the popular view of a selected area
and since I'm in the conservative southeast of America
I am thrust into a world in which I am a flashing neon sign
bull's-eye already tattooed on my back
should I abide by prohibitions that have long eroded
in more developed areas of the country?
or should I resist and fight for the ability to be myself
without fear or shame?
Damn right. fight.
I'll never conform to your close-minded views and self-tyranny
I will liberate myself from your fascist democracy.

037

Women.
Women are wonderful.
Women make living enjoyable.
At least seemly.
Women make suicide seem not an option.
Women.
Not the nagging trailer trash women.
Who chain smoke and have children
As their formal occupation
But the real women.
Something about a woman's voice
That can elevate me into another level.
Another dimension.
Women dominate every aspect
From an underground stance.
Very clever, very sneaky.
But understandable.
Women are the force from inertia
That pushes any evolution.
They are the reason
We males build and create.
We cater to the obsession
That women allow us privilege.
So we take forth on the quest
Of enchanting by any ridiculous means necessary.
I'm sexist.
I hate males.
I hate me.

038

Everything's already been done
So why repeat it?
Well we could say the love story
Has been driven far into the ground
Beaten to death
Used up beyond repair or recognition
But how can we discard it?
Then Hollywood movies
And country and pop songs
Would become non-existent
Words are just words
Wrap them up in decorative disguises
But everything's getting cliché
And no story is truly "original"
Thus you have second rate, second hand imitation
And nothing will change
So embrace the literary fate
The fake portrayal of society
Set in words to confuse and falsify
The next generation to come
The world's on repeat…

039

less than a year to go
on this tragic wasteland
nothing but dry sand
from here on out
becoming more at peace
with myself
with my destiny
my eyelids are heavier
from constant consciousness
memory flooded with dullness
no inspiration
lack of interest in anything
all the thrills are gone
used up, rotted away
music doesn't get me
almost chore-like
movies bore me
all collections on hold
tv is long obsolete
radio is not even any option
books are too time consuming
sex – my mind throbs it
my body won't allow it
internet is the new soul-stealer
but my attention drifts
again to the nothingness
empty in this hollow frame
this begins the countdown…

040

Crazed and exhausted from catching too many falling stars.
The blisters burst after awhile and the fluid runs down the conscience.
Mental projections evoke physical brutality.
Breathe in whatever you choose, consume freely.
The air needs filtering because the fallopian tubes are starting to rust.
Scribble me a new sky.
The dullness puts a blackhead on a pimple on a blemish.
Can't nature take its course without a kick in the ass?
Never question the questions. ? .
Wash the dirty brain with preprograms and watch the smile adjust itself.
Having sex with sadness could erode your genitalia.
The razor won't make it go away.
What point is this pointed at the dome?
Just another victim of over-exposure.
A candle light vigil for untapped potential.
General census is edible regurgitation.
Growing into regression may be the healthiest method to survive.
Godspeed like the flash and remember to wipe the grime away.
Only to battle with another day.
Words from the heavy burdened lungs of your favorite wordsmith.

041

What position will the fantasy entail today?
New love will lubricate the soul if it's worn and squeaky
But may leave a bad after taste.
Allergic to happiness is common.
Pick your goal and run forward.
Fractured splints won't hold back fate.
Nevertheless keep running into traffic.
If the egg breaks then forget fertilization.
Check the equipment status to update or downsize.
But never loan a thought to a fickle friend.
Wax and buffer? Maybe a drink first.
Truly deep these lines form on the surface
Yet beneath it rips through bone.
My god, does anybody know how lonely I am right now?
Forget the vulnerable outbursts
They leak out from time to time.
The season has turned and twisted the inner wall of tissue.
Login to your new personality.
No one will ever suspect the truth.
Lurid are the tales to tickle the fancy.
Does this make me a pervert?
My, the sun has set its last.
Lock up the cages, kids.
First we must die to be reborn.
Wait until the fall.
Damn these cannibals are tasty.
Somebody really should break my hands
To halt this madness.

042

ah, the politics of a pretty girl
so special, queen of the world
you are the most exquisite…wait…
I can't write this…
does being pretty make you special?
society says yes, I say no
a pretty face, a sexy body
yeah it's a gift
but if that's your finest quality,
then you probably aren't much fun
sure you'll have legions of followers
bowing before you, hoping to sample your beauty
I'm not going to be all stoic and moralistic here
so if you're a good looking girl
sure I want you in my bed
but can you make impressions in my head
you can always spot the special ones
but not by appearances alone
they are water marked by a strange aura
yet over time the signs got misinterpreted
transformed into a showcase for marketing
and now every pretty girl thinks she's unique
an image fed by her minions
what grand illusions we endure…

043

circumcised this love
wrap me in fine linen
take over the reins
life-sized monkey hugs

customize your gloves
trap me in your denim
rake over the pains
night eyes of day doves

lobotomize from above
zap me into a demon
break over the grain
bite-sized deadly drugs

desensitize this love
rape me in fine linen
take hold the reins
half-sized money thugs

044

Sometimes I don't understand at all
Sometimes I wish I didn't feel so small
Is the girl in your head the girl in your heart?
Is the girl in your dreams the girl in your bed?

Another wonderful Saturday night all alone
Listen to albums to hear a voice other than my own

If love could just be love, but no
That would be too easy
Mix jealousy, domination, grief, and uncompromising differences
And you end up with a leap not worth the risk
…I'll fight so hard to get you just to throw you away
… I was sentimental once

I can't think of life as a missed opportunity
I can't do everything you do
And if I could, would I want to?

It's my lifetime
But how much of it is actually mine?

Nothing can save you now
This time the dream will end
I won't let you inside my world…anymore

What'll you say when they take all their titles away?
Does no recognition mean no existence?

Tired. The kind of tired that rest doesn't cure.

045

Why are you
The way you are
I know my mind
Can't be that far
Away from you
From your view
So I don't
Know why you choose
To do that
Stupid shit you do
You make the mockery
You are the fool.

Here's to you
I hope you have a happy breakdown
When the break-up breaks you down to the ground
Cause if you've never felt that ache inside
Then you don't know that you're really alive

I've been on both sides of this tug-of-war
Now it's your turn
And once you get this far down there's no u-turn
Descend and feel the breeze as you burn

Last night I had an intimate funeral for you
I know you're not really dead
But you're dead to my life…

My sweat becomes your sweat
My fluids become your fluids

Don't define me by what I do
I'm nothing to most, I'm nothing to you
You were the platform I embraced, with a grip to hold on
Now you're not a savior to me, the illusion is gone…

046

Be who you want

I saw you today
Standing out in the rain
Acting so unprotected
Like you weren't affected
But I know that deep down you are dying
In need of someone to come through and save you, stop your crying
Why can't that someone be me?
Would that be too easy?
Life slips away
Everyday
You sit around with him
And you waste away
If you come with me
I would set you free
And you can finally be
Who you want to be
I saw you again
Tonight talking to the wind
Whispering little prayers
Meanwhile I am still right here
Life slips away
Everyday
You sit around with him
And you waste away
If you come with me
I would set you free
And you can finally be
Who you want to be
You want this I know
Close your eyes and let go…
But I know that deep down you are dying
In need of someone to come through and save you, stop your crying
Why can't that someone be me?
Would that be too easy?
Life slips away
Everyday
You sit around with him
And you waste away
If you come with me
I would set you free
And you can finally be
Who you want to be

047

How do you make me shake so?
When will this hold let go and stay gone?
Every time you come by me
Weirdness engulfs my energy
All it takes is one look
All it takes is one time
All it takes is one glace
And once again you dig in my mind
Why, why do I
Still have a reaction
Still have an attraction
To you
How can you be so cruel?
How can you be so naive?
How can you be so sexy?
How are you the only girl I'll ever need?
All it takes is one look
All it takes is one time
All it takes is one glace
And once again you dig in my mind
Why, why do I
Still have a reaction
Still have an attraction
To you
The butterflies that align my stomach wall
Let me know that you can be found not far
With a word or a single smile
I'm right back at the starting point
I still wonder…
Why, why do I
Still have a reaction
Still have an attraction
To you

048

I would like to have someone who couldn't live without me
Someone, who at my destruction, literally couldn't continue
The devastation would overwhelm and would succeed me
A beautiful union that cannot survive separately

…
but I'll never have that.

In the movies when lovers split it becomes a blood feud
Usually ending in the demise of one by the hands of assassinators
Or brutal domesticated murder
But in real life it isn't that plot (well, occasionally)
But usually it's just a lot of tears and lonely hours and sad songs
And old movies and more tears.

From here on out I won't write about the soul
Because I don't have it contained
I won't write about hearts unless it's the literal term
Because there's no use using euphuisms
I won't write about the stars
and how I'd pull them down for you
Besides they're overrated anyway
I won't write about giving you the world
Because it's not mine to give
I won't write about always being good for you
Because I'm not always nice
And you know what?
Hearts don't look like hearts
And stars don't look like stars
So you may look like the one
But how will I really know?

049

I scrawl down words hastily caught
A patchwork quilt of bleary blunt thought
A cluster of disaster in my mind
Lament laminated over time
Straying away from any sanity
Cannon fodder for my depravity
To grow old and decrepit
To be nursed, fed, and helpless
A fear that's running rampant
A vow never to achieve that
Take an oath of non-celibacy
Leave occupation out the home scene
Try to make my time simple
Happily licking nail polished nipples
Fighting inside for control of the gun
Everything is pointless, nothing in everyone
Needing a nightcap, cap off the night
Can't readily decide who I want at my side
Dark and brooding, mood set in stone
All is lost, my life on hold
Jet lag without even riding a plane
Seasick in the desert, clouded without rain
Nothing is planned, unsure what's next
Above any demographs and test subjects
Thinking positive as to be disappointed
Thinking one day I'll be well rewarded
No longer be the bottom feeder of before
There is no glitter girl, no one to adore
We all have a whore inside, being deprived
I am the unclaimed consolation prize
Having an allergic reaction to life
Having nothing left to write
Alter myself before I get too weird
So here's a period to end this period here.

050

the sad thing about beautiful beginnings
is that they always come to violent ends

---

today I woke up suffocating
do I need sedating or is it the girl I'm dating?

I'm tired of everything, all this stale commercial hypnosis
I don't care if it feels good, I don't care if it feels bad
I just want to feel something

We tie ourselves up, chain ourselves down
So we can howl at the moon

I would be the one who would scream "fuck you" to the moon but I
wouldn't cuss in front of your mother because I have respect.
Maybe that separates me from peers but who are peers anyway?
Every time I've peered into the abyss, I see nothing…

I believe love is a chemical reaction because your hands
don't make me shake like they did a month before

---

put yourself outside the box and realize that you can't rely on
another's perspectives to form any objective rationalization
be it a person, thing, or an idea, opinionate yourself
and fear not the cost

We all have a fear of being doomed to repeat the mistakes of our ancestry

---

why do dreams need to be chased?

I think girls have sex with me in the hopes that I'll write about them
But in turn I have written to seduce…

Darkness

side

a view that burrows deep into the chaotic horror of infested imagination and stirs up the demons that sleep within.

01

Another night, darkness reigns
Engulfed by empty aches in veins
Allowing torturing thoughts to fall
Consuming the lust to lose it all
Please, no exposure to the light
Even a 60 watt will be too bright
These eyes squint, too bloodshot to see
All the wicked terror that befalls me
Now thc blood runs everywhere
I like to watch it disappear
Into the cracks onto the floor below
The neighbors will never know
Why this room is stained so red
And how the demons control my head
Leading me to destruction and pain
My actions made don't feel deranged
Finding internal pleasure by external means
One of the lucky to live out my dreams
Such fantasies invoke my inner spirits
The sweetest song yet only I hear it
Now morning creeps back stealing time
Must close out this fun of mine
Shut my eyes, underneath a pillow
Maybe at dusk I won't be so low
With a bash or with a slice
Tonight another roll of dice
Wake up with a certain hint of gloom
Then paint with blood, this empty room.

02

I could murder someone
Anyone
Sometimes I'd like to everyone
Get them out of my sight
People piss me off
In their predictable little uniforms
Untied in ignorance
Skin them alive
To show them their frailty
No mercy awarded
Laugh as the liquid drips
Standing in the puddle
On the descended pancreas pile
I'll have a demented smile
All men are created evil
The breaking point is near
Unleash on someone
Anyone
Take it out on everyone
Within immediate surroundings
Victims at random
They're better off
I'm their savior
They should thank me
With their final breath.

03

I'm caught in your web
Your trap
Kidnapped
Led me to this cage
In this cave
Where no one will hear
My screams
My cries
My wrists so scraped and bruised
Tired of standing in one spot
The light is a crack in the wall
A faint gleam of escape
Taunting me with a false hope
Been a captive too long
I'll never see freedom again
Accustomed to your torture
Such violence from soft hands
Such hideous words from glossy lips
I'm caught in your web
Spinning me inside out
Sticky like an alien womb
You crawl to me
Take a quick bite
Then scurry back to the corner
While I wince
In pleasurable pain
Seduced into submission
By the Queen of Pain
That angel disguise tricked me good
Threw out the caution
Now I'm rotting
In my own fermented stenches
While she bathes before me
Giving me a full view
Before she bludgeons me unconscious
To awaken hours later …alone.

04

how to explain to you
the change in me
who you knew before
is not who you now see
one day feelings came
could no longer be myself
a short period transformation
morphed into something else
instantly I threw away
any ideas I'd been saving
this morning I awoke
with a new relentless craving
all my yesterdays are dead
forever numbed and gone
you may have gave me birth
but I am not your son.

05

At the arcades, playing Castlevania II
When I met you, little sexy ghoul
Black hair, black clothes, black make-up
Later in the restroom, we're playing make-out
Rings here and there, tattoos on white skin
Wrapped those thin legs around me, dug your heels in
Curled out your tongue, offered me some
Couldn't resist as you bit me hard for fun
You laughed so did I, revealing a darker side
Living for the moment, knowing soon we will die
Lipstick on my shirt, my hand under your skirt
Your nails scratch until I couldn't feel the hurt
We stood amazed at our own impulsive ways
We're the children of forsaken dreams but it's o.k.
Blindly we push forward into a future unseen
Where elders already accomplished everything
But we strive to adapt and survive
We'll find methods to let them know we're alive
As we left the stall, with no number to call
My sexy ghoul and I went different paths and that was all.

06

Lovely love at my side
You could be my blushing bride
You could bring this deadness to life
But all I can offer you is the night
Only a vicious and hypnotic sight
But would you stay at my side
Knowing the things in which I take pride
Knowing the emptiness inside
When the hunger's too strong to hide
Can you handle that nocturnal drive
Or would you leave me here to die
Bring the blinding sun to these eyes
That's a chance I can't take tonight
so hold your breath love and say goodbye

07

fresh kill
flesh kill
feast on this
drain me
maim me
a rainstorm kiss
cut me
gut me
inject disease
rip in
new sin
comes with ease
just bone
no tone
recluse next door
so weird
you're scared
blood on the floor ?
carcass
car crash
screams unheard
deliberate
accident
spoken not a word.

08

I am an introverted vampire
Instead of living forever
I've never really lived at all
Instead of needing blood
From an outside source
I must release the blood
That already exists in my veins

Instead of feeding
From the living
I hide away in the shadows
Avoiding any connection
Instead of feeling the thirst
I feel nothing
A truly dead undead

09

Bat fetish, spider phobia
Death is on the way
Becoming more of less
Become more lifeless everyday

Mortal man, immortal love
Lusting so Neanderthal
Spiked punch, spiked collar
Lips that can do it all

Bat fetish, spider phobia
Mayhem in the air
Blooms that are found frozen
With not a soul to care

10

Welcome to the Grand Guignol
Formerly known as my life
What I can't say with words
I'll say with this knife

Time masks the countdown
The final hours of consciousness
In that time all the values are weighted
What really matters gets lost in grey matter
And the ability to understand is a curse
Luckily few obtain that torture

So cold
But everything feels better
In the dark
In the dark of night
Can't take it in the light
It feels better in the dark
The only way to stay alive
Feels better in the dark
In the dark of night

11

We are all creators and destroyers in our own way.
We fuel that fire that burns our frigid fingers.
We rest our weary wants on bloody rusted hooks.
We are all in this watcherless playground together.
We are connected by our own inevitable omega.

Where individuality has no backing.
Where every accomplishment fades away.
Where the society's classes are indistinguishable.
Where time renders every previous word or action pointless.
Where no one keeps score and no one wins.

In the end, nothing really matters at all.
In the end, all the great problems are small.
In the end, time is but a joke.
In the end, there is no faith in hope.
In the end, we disappear into the vast abyss like a speck of sand
or a cloud of smoke.

12

All the blood
Runs over me
All the hits
Bruise memory
All the breaths
Gulps of air
All the want
Forfeited dare
All the ache
Deep in bone
All the trust
Forever gone
All the nerve
Bound of steel
All the lies
Protective shield
All the dreams
Never same
All the rain
Stored up pain
All the days
What a waste
All the tears
Their salty taste
All the love
Forgot to give
All the life
Forgot to live
All the talk
Overheard
All the paths
Seeming absurd
All the death
That steals hope
All the reasons
To hang from this rope

13

Best friends
Worst enemies
Torn apart
Over the love
Of a girl

Love destroys
Love forms hate
After time
Misery intertwined
Her conscience
Forces suicide

A note found
With final words:

"I gave my blood
I gave my love
I poured my tears
I poured my blood
Chance and risk
My greed atone
Eagerly to obtain
Now left alone
No repenting
For damage done
Love is a war
That hate has won
I erase this
Competition prize
I cut these wrists
And close these eyes"

14

be my pumpkin,
this Halloween
I'll carve you up,
I'll make you scream

be my pumpkin
I'll trick and treat
serving sliced chunks
of gruesome meat

be my pumpkin
deadness of night
you will give off
a glowing orange light

be my pumpkin
delight for a day
until tomorrow
when I throw you away

15

well kiddies and kitties
looks like the gauntlet has been thrown
a few meters at least
(motherfucker's heavy)
the day breaks on mistakes
and the vile battle wages on
with a split of the tongue (for fun?)
and the guts are gross
wrapped around the sharp posts
and hey you never know
could end up on your toast
what a tasty dish and wind is so brisk
dying for the prayers to grant a death wish
blood is the river flowing down the liver
running down the thigh that's why you should never
keep your corpses under your bed
those carpet stains are dark muddy red
but the time is short when death is the sport
yes that quiet guy isn't quiet inside
inside the plotting, planning of demise
see the destruction within his cold eyes
he goes unnoticed and unheard
and without saying a word
says Everything
everything you will come to believe
right before you die
all reasons and whys
you'll step back and retract
paralyzed look intact
and quietly like the boy you'll slip into the black
the black yes the black
where there's no turning back
nothing to gain but filling the cracks
under the dirt and the grime
as you're guaranteed it's a wonderful time
what's left behind, from this thing called your mind
a speck of dust in the pile and you thought it divine.

16

The dissection of the vivisection of my fatal death
A quarter and two – joined the exclusive club
- in my head so many times
All throughout the year
And in ways, parts of me did die
Parts of life broken and abandoned
Shedding and shredding exoskeleton
Yet here I sit - a day beyond
The culminated pinnacle of my adolescent dream
A vow at 15, broken at 28
A gutted trout flipping on dry land
What tomorrow holds
I don't plan, I don't want, don't yearn for
I'll just stumble forward
Until I discover a reason to halt this forever descent
I survived – my worst nightmare
My worst nightmare – I survived
Failed my mission
My punishment is to remain exiled in hell
A walking corpse, truly living dead
Maybe I'm on a grace period
And the new me will exploit ambitions I've only dreamed about
Maybe I'll uncover a smile somewhere
Maybe this is my second chance
Or maybe I'm just gutless, bloodless, fallible fool - a hollow shame
Dear me, I'm sorry… unforgivable letdown to a shattered goal.

17

A hero
That's what I wanted to be
Yet it's becoming too apparent
That there is evil inside
A dark force within
Driving the motion of emotion
Pushing me into constant friction
The seesaw in my mind
Wanting to aid those in need
From a cause unknown
Save the population
The population I resist
I desist from adapting
No attendance to their meetings
No connection to the masses
No way to solve their problems
No hero
Merely a self-destructive quarantine
No powers
No talent and no ability
No agenda but suffering
The pain and hate and hurt
All I have to give
So take from me
Sweet misery
Or nothing at all
I'm not a villain ...really
But I'm filled with a raging despair
That will choke the air
Out of any mortal human
Cursed to inflict without intent
What a gift.

18

death death and more death
death is all I know
my only constant
"the all engulfing"
my grandfather was
all in all, a good man
with many friends
and loved ones
but his last few years
were terribly painful
and he remained
with limited movement
almost bedridden
yet the old man
was a struggling survivor
he still had his mind
although occasionally
a bit of senility
would seep through
when my grandmother (his wife)
proceeded him 2 years before
townspeople had their rumors
claiming he'd give in to the loss
and find his eternal sleep
not the case at all
he fought for his life
in and out of hospitals
not until he was admitted
into a nursing facility
did he finally succumb
after being left alone
by everyone he loved
he let go and passed on
leaving a memory of life
for those who knew
and I'm left here
to feel remorse
and to question the value
the purpose of it all
as all motivation fades
I feel disgust
for this pathetic planet
I feel helpless and hopeless
like nothing I do will matter
I want to sleep
I want to rest myself - undisturbed.
can't play this game any longer.

19

The couple just finishing having sex
They laid there in the dark
The sweat still clinging
To their exhausted bodies
Suddenly her urethra
Starts erupting like a volcano
Her vagina is a desert of fire
She twitches trying to calm it
Nothing works
Finally she jumps up out of bed
Runs to the bathtub
Turns on the cold water
Hand laps it onto her crotch
She looks to investigate
Her pubic area is blood red
Her whole pelvic region is frying
To a crisp and disintegrating
Running down her thigh
She sees red marks
Marks of inflamed semen
He said he used a condom
He lied
She falls over in shock and dies
In the bedroom he watches TV
Smokes a cigarette and smiles
He was diagnosed with toxic semen
Fatally harmful to the recipients
Nearly four months ago
He vowed to NOT have intercourse
A lie of course
In fact
That's all he's been doing lately
Fucking and leaving
His selection is random
Any girl will do
Sex kills is too easily the ironic tag for this story.

"Duplicity"

"Trying to love two women is like a ball and chain"... And that situation gets even stickier when you are unaware of it. Buford Blankenship, a successful record storeowner and part time poet, had a rare condition that he wasn't even really aware of. Well, of course he knew he had blackouts and certain elapses of memory but he didn't know that in those unaccountable hours he was most definitely conscious. Schizophrenia, as it turns out, had been in Buford's lineage in every 3rd generation. Neither his father nor grandfather had the disorder.

Buford was a well-to-do gentleman and was as mild mannered as a chivalrous knight from the time of King Arthur. He had a nice apartment in the southeastern part of town just north of the Roaming Hills. At 25 years of age, he also found himself madly in love with a lovely mall clerk named Veronica. She was a radiant ball of sunshine. They had a very healthy and passionate relationship. But unbeknownst to both of them, an evil secret was enveloping within Buford.

When he suddenly "dies for awhile," Buford has a major transformation. Another personality completely encompasses his body and his regular persona is seemingly lost somewhere in limbo. Milo, the dark and free spirited side of Mr. Blankenship, surfaces and runs amok in the carefully built life of Buford. Milo has less regard for rules and structure. He likes to go to the local bars and clubs where he mixes it up with the ladies looking for an alleviation from loneliness. He drinks way too much and uses profanities like they were the only words in the English language. One night in a crummy dive, he saw a woman wearing all gothic attire while swaying to the ear piercing music from a band that sounded like it could have been their first practice together. After sparking conversation as the drinks were consumed, Milo invited the strikingly sexy brunette, Erika, over to his apartment for more permeation. This continued for months as Milo grew to adore this uninhibited sex goddess. She always left before sunrise so Buford would arise fully unaware of the proceeding night's events.

Until one morning, when Buford's jaw dropped hard at the sight of a nude stranger lying next to him as he awoke. His heart beat even faster when Veronica paid him a surprise visit that morning. She stood in shock briefly before yelling "fucking asshole" as her body

"Duplicity"

started to convulse in heartbreak. He turned to the woman not knowing her name and said, "Please leave". She put on her pants and button-up blouse while carrying her undergarments and sadomasochistic accessories. Buford pleaded with Veronica but there was to be no reconciliation. She told him it was completely over. Buford was devastated.

A few nights later he came home drunk and passed out before he could reach his bed. When Milo surfaced, he searched the bars and found Erika already attached to another lover, this time a female. Milo, not having the calm, cool, collectedness of Buford, went home and began to cry. Having two separate heartbreaks at once, agony overcame all rationalization. Milo scribbled a note and drank a shot of whiskey. He went into the closet and got the 9-millimeter that was there for protection. He thought of Erika but for some reason a blonde was appearing in his head as well. With one last gulp of alcohol and one last breath of misery, Milo turned the gun on himself and shot a hole through the back of his head. Blood ran everywhere, completely redecorating the tile. And as with one stone getting two birds, one bullet ends two entirely different lives.

"Ojibwa Way"

It was a mild and sunny day in the northern part of Crestview, Florida. He, with his slim tanned frame adorned with 4 tattoos: 2 tribal designs, a bar code, and a demon-like winged creature, pulled into his driveway after a long night's work down at the local power plant. It wasn't his dream but it was decent money. He threw the keys habitually on the glass coffee table and pushed the play button on his answering machine. The girl that he loved left a message in a sobbing voice: "I'm sorry…I can't take this anymore …I love you but I don't know how you feel…if you want to keep me here meet me at the beach in Pensacola…be there by 2:00p.m. or I'm leaving for good…I hope you're there…just make the effort". They had had a terrible dissension the day before and it was left unresolved. She had been given the opportunity to further her studies of ancient art, her passion since she was a child, abroad. Although she desperately wanted to go, she couldn't fathom the thought of leaving him behind. They had discussed it a few weeks previous and she had decided to forfeit or at least postpone her chance to travel overseas. Lately they were quarreling over a previous love interest of hers, with whom she still worked, and also his inability to communicate effectively in a loving manner.

When he heard those words from the static filled speaker, his heart sank like a thrown anchor and he panicked in a way he had never felt before. With all the nervous tension, he fumbled back to the table to grab his keys and headed out to prevent the only one he loved from leaving and leaving him with an empty space that he could never fill. His breaths were short and heavy as he got in his car and headed to highway 90 en route to Pensacola. Although he needed a shave and a shower, his thoughts were preoccupied with reclaiming and renouncing his love to the girl of his dreams. On highway 90, the traffic was extremely thick as workers were on their lunch break going to and fro. He tried to pass to gain ground but found that he couldn't for all the oncoming vehicles.

He seemed to be stuck behind a little gray Sedan that was going much slower than the speed limit suggests. The car was an older model and had collected quite a bit of dust, so much in fact that he could barely make out the license plate. Yet with a little squinting he read the numbers 120-981 and the county of Monroe. Although he had never been there, he was roughly familiar with the area of the Florida Keys. Through the back glass of the Sedan, he could see in the rearview mirror what appeared to be a small elderly lady, wearing big brown glasses and a pink scarf adorned with yellow flowers around her head. With tires screeching and brakes grinding, he tried again and again to make his way around the old woman who seemed to be enjoying the sites very carefully and in no hurry at all. Honking the horn in fury accomplished nothing. His road

"Ojibwa Way"

rage was at the boiling point as he realized his chances of stopping his love from leaving lessened and lessened. He tried his cell phone but he wasn't getting a signal. He threw it against the dashboard and cursed at the slow turtle-like driver before him. His head hit the steering wheel in distraught acknowledgement of his unfortunate circumstances.

She was standing on the sandy shores of Pensacola Beach holding her luggage, a plane ticket, and passport in her hand. The soft wind was blowing her radiant red hair gently over her face as she gazed out at the dark blue mass of water. Down deep, she wanted him to stop her, to give her a reason for staying in Crestview. He had been the only one who seemed to truly understand her and for that she felt connected in a way like she had never known. The day before when they had met for lunch and were discussing certain issues, he seemed much more out of tune with her than usual. The topics were ones always rehashed whenever she talked about her work because he hated the fact that she worked along side her ex-boyfriend and his insecurities always got the best of him. His gentle hands become fists and his eyes contained a rage that she hadn't seen before. She wanted him to just express himself to show her that she was the one he wanted. Admittedly, some times she would bring up her previous lover to cause the jealousy, which to her evoked a certain amount of caring, in him to surface. Yesterday was different somehow. He responded in forceful aggression that led her to question their future. With a sarcastic hateful tone, he said, "Why don't you just go to France. I think we'd both be better off." That bitter comment led her to give him an ultimatum of meeting her on the beach and working things out or letting her go alone to a strange land where she would make a new start. With the last draw off of her last cigarette, she looked at her watch that read 1:45p.m.

Meanwhile, back on highway 90, he continues driving at the speed of 35 mph behind the snail woman. She turns on her right turn signal and, in another 10 minutes, she finally turns off the road allowing him to accelerate as he races to the northwestern tip of Florida. Upon arriving at the beach, he immediately scurried to the sand where dozens of couples and families were basking in the warm sunshine. He did a 360-degree search but didn't see any sign of his beautiful confidante. His head hung low as he released a deep sigh of defeat. Suddenly he realized his last chance to track her down. She would've gone to the Pensacola airport to begin her journey. He ran to his car and headed on interstate 10 to the Pensacola airport.

Although he searched every waiting room and boarding line in the entire facility after arriving, it was obvious that he had failed his mission.

"Ojibwa Way"

He went back to his two-bedroom house with gray siding in Crestview and sat alone staring blankly off into space. He held a picture of the two of them together taken a year previously when they had spent almost a whole day at the state fair. Now those days seemed lost forever. Within the next few weeks he tried to contact her but couldn't figure out a way to reach her all the way on the other side of the world. Finally, months later when he was doing some cleaning he found a letter of acceptance addressed from the school overseas. With a few calls he received a number that had her name attached to it. With clammy hands that shook with nervous fear, he dialed the digits and waited to hear that angelic voice which had for too long evaded him. As he gasped and clinched his teeth, a voice answered on the other end. It was not the voice he was expecting. A deep masculine voice said in a groggy tone, "Bonjour". After a long pause he put the receiver down and hung up the phone. He fell back on his queen size bed and looked up at the ceiling. A moment later he stood and with blood racing began an anarchic fit of emotion that culminated in him ripping down every picture, poster, and pinned up reminder of her. His head was exploding with pain and a thousand images were slide-showing in his brain but through it all he could see one sight very vividly: the Monroe County license plate 120-981.

2 years later

In the warm humid climate of the southern most part of the United States also known as the Florida Keys, it was a typical day in the suburban part of Monroe County. Key Largo is a well known tourist attraction but just outside the diving posts and marinas there are quiet little communities where many people come to retire or to get away from the city life. Deep in the heart of this suburb lived a retired gentleman by the name of Trevor Wendorff. He lived alone because his remaining family had little to do with him. Although married once upon a time, Trevor never had any children. His only social activity was the weekly bingo game tournament held at the local community center. He would parade around humming the tune "Knoxville Girl". Then he would sit and talk to all the senior citizens that joined him.

After a long session of bingo, Trevor came back home and took a mid-day nap. When he awoke, it was dark out. Trevor switched on a nearby lamp and felt around his chair for the remote. Digging it out of the side pocket, he turned on the television to catch the evening news. A few minutes into the program, there was a special bulletin about a killer who is apparently stalking and murdering people within the community.

"Ojibwa Way"

Police said that all the victims were elderly. Trevor watched in horror as they showed eight different incidents of homicide. **1:** a seventy-one year old male with severe emphysema had his respiratory equipment destroyed and the phone line cut. **2 & 3:** a sixty-nine year old female and her seventy-three year old husband had been set on fire. Not their home just themselves. They ran outside but burned alive. Their water supply had been tampered with and blocked from use. **4:** an eighty-three year old woman had been punched to death, breaking nearly every fragile bone in her body. **5:** a seventy-six year old woman was thrown from a three-story window railing at a housing complex. She landed on hard concrete and died instantly. **6:** a man ninety-one years of age was tied up, castrated, and left to bleed to death. **7 & 8:** an eighty-nine year old female and a male, 101 years old, were forced to have intercourse while they were tied together in the missionary position. The killer forced them to copulate as carbon monoxide slowly filled the room. "The police are still investigating the…"

Suddenly the power goes off in Trevor's apartment. He got up out of his recliner and peered out his window. No storm brewing outside. All his neighbors still had power in their homes. Trevor decided it must be a blown fuse. He grabbed a flashlight from the dresser drawer and made his way into the bedroom. Opting to fix the fuse tomorrow, Trevor lit a candle on the table near his bed. He switched off the flashlight and began to pull back the covers. Then out of nowhere the killer silently stalks closer. The killer grabs Trevor by the neck and holds him from behind. After a fierce struggle, Trevor kicks his opponent in the crotch and picked up the candle to get a better view of his attacker. Yet when Trevor turned around, he saw no one. Suddenly the light from the candle went out and Trevor froze silently in terror. Hoping his predator would go away, he tried not to breathe. Then all of a sudden he found it hard to. The killer stole the candle from Trevor's hand and shoved the entire nine inches of wax down his throat. Trevor gasped and fought, but was eventually overpowered. A neighbor found the body two days later. The candle wax had hardened inside Trevor's mouth.

Elsewhere in the world: someone selects and buys a gun. Then someone purchases a plane ticket.

A week after Trevor's tragic demise, the news had put the community on full alert. Everyone began locking all doors and windows as well as taking extra precautionary measures to ensure their safety. A curfew was set to keep everyone indoors after dark.

The Monroe County Retirement Home and Nursing Facility houses about 350 senior citizens who come to receive care and to be around others of similar age. It was a place where the elderly felt safe and understood. The power went out in the middle of the night and everyone started to panic. The two guards staffed at the facility began to investigate the blackout while nurses and orderlies tried to maintain composure in order to calm the patients. With everyone preoccupied, the killer went from room to room, slicing through the elderly as they lay sleeping. Some were awake but weren't disturbed by the appearance in their rooms because the killer had stolen and was wearing an orderly uniform and was pretending to bring water to the patients. Those awake would be gagged and then slit with a razor sharp knife. The killer continued to prey upon the victims until the guards finally caught sight of the stranger. The killer ran down the dark hallway and hid until the guards passed. Then silently backtracking to the fire escape where first entered, the killer exited quickly. The guards called the police but by the time they arrived the killer was gone. No clues were left. One hundred and thirty-five of the residents of the convalescent home were murdered. Most were due to blood loss. Two other patients died of heart attacks caused by the traumatic shock of the horrorific event.

A few nights later the killer leaves a dim dingy apartment room and drives throughout the suburbs looking for something. Driving from street to street inspecting very carefully. This has been the routine for months now. Then all of a sudden the car comes to a complete stop. The killer steps out of the vehicle and stealth walks up behind a Lexus car parked in the carport of a two-story brick home. There were lights on in the house and there was another car in the driveway. The killer was only interested in the Lexus. Actually, just the license plate. The number was **120-981**, the same as on the gray Sedan two years previous. Yes, the killer was the guy who lost his girl when he couldn't catch her in time. He blamed his unfortunate luck on the slow old lady driver. Now he wanted his revenge and he's been taking it out on every elderly person he has come in contact with. He felt as though he was doing humanity a service by eliminating the weaker links. Now he had found the correct number he had been searching for. Yet the car was wrong though. He had to be sure. Getting a general layout of the structure, he climbed up to the second story where he could enter through a window, hopefully without alerting the owners. With little effort, he cut a hole in the glass and opened the hatch. Once inside he began to look for clues that might somehow assure him the old woman lived here. He was getting satisfaction by killing other victims but just not enough. He had to tie up this loose end once and for all. The dresser drawer turned up fruitless. A lot of old clothes but nothing to pinpoint exactly. The room definitely had that "old lady" smell to it. He went through various possessions to no avail. Then he opened the closet. The darkness allowed little light. He used his pocket flashlight to see inside.

"Ojibwa Way"

Going through dresses, skirts, and tops, when he stopped. Finally he had found a clue. The clue. The pink scarf with yellow flowers she wore on that fateful day. The memory of it was burned forever in his mind. He had found her at last. Tonight would conclude his reign of terror, he thought to himself. Now to execute his plan. He slowly turned the doorknob to exit the room, careful not to be heard or seen. The hallway was clear as he silently stepped to the staircase. He could see the light from a room on the bottom floor. Taking his time, he made his way down the stairs and stood before the room with light coming from it. Although he could hear voices in the distance, he couldn't make out what was being said. He held the scarf tightly between his hands and prepared to battle until her death. With stamina gathered, he lunged into the room. Making his way around a corner, he turned to see the short little woman standing near a kitchen table. He drew back the scarf, preparing to strangle his target when something caught the corner of his eye. He turned his head clockwise and froze in shock. There stood the woman he dearly loved, bewildered and screaming. Everything happened in slow motion from there. The girl who left him behind was right in front of him, moving forward with an agonized look upon her face. Slowly he turned toward the old lady and to his surprise found her aiming a pistol to his chest area.

As he turned to disarm her, he gave one last look at the woman all of this had been about in the first place. He wondered how and why she was there. Then it was too late. As he completed his turn, the old woman fired two shots into his chest cavity. He fell to the ground, scarf still in hand. "Grandma no!" the young girl cried out. "I'm sorry," she said to him as he lay dying. "So sorry."

Apparently the young woman had heard about the tragic events occurring from her apartment overseas and proceeded to bring her grandmother a gun to protect herself from any would be assailant. Little did she know that the killer was her ex-boyfriend. As he lay there cold and still, she felt a deep remorse and sympathy toward him.

Now everything had come full circle. He had never met her grandparents so he was completely unaware of the connection. Her grandmother had been to Crestview that day to see her off and was heading back to the Keys when he got behind her. The ironic fate was that her grandmother unknowingly prevented the couple from staying together. Now with a gun she severed the connection for good. He was gone and the terror was over. The grandmother called the police and the mystery murders were finally solved. The young woman returns overseas to her fiancée's while her grandmother lives on to eventually die a heroine of Macon County.

"Ma Cobb"

I awoke in the mid afternoon with a throbbing headache still intact. The woods provided the necessary cover to shield me from any possible predator. I have been out here for 5 days straight with only berries to eat and creek water to drink. The fatigue is overpowering often times, yet I must continue forward. My leg is injured from the escape and the dried blood is stained on these ragged clothes. Then I heard a noise. I held my breath as I stood frozenly still. A soft stepping broke some branches on the ground and then suddenly stopped. Being startled with heart racing, I hid behind a large tree and peered slowly to see my attacker. A sigh of relief came when I saw merely a doe, female deer, simply standing in silence. I then returned to my fleeing. After crossing many hills and countless acres of forest, I finally saw light through the trees as I approached a dirty path where people obviously travel often. I walked miles and miles it seemed, without any sign of human life. Exhaustion wore me out and I slumped down alongside the path and fell asleep.

When I came to, I was in a town hospital and a doctor and sheriff were there to question me. Apparently the sheriff had found me unconscious and brought me to the hospital to examine my injuries. At first, I didn't know where to begin. They asked me my name. "My name is Vlandon. I live in the Black Bare region at the Cobb farm." The officer volunteered to take me home when the doctor released me. "No" I screamed. "You can't take me back there." "Why not," the sheriff inquired. "Because …" I said as I took a deep breath.

"Many years ago there was a young lady named Martha Cobb. She was poorly educated and never had many friends. Her mother entered her in all the beauty contests in the local town from an infant to a teenager. She never won once and this left a devastating effect on her psyche. Born with a defective central nervous system, Martha had a nervous twitch and her eyes roamed separately as if each had a life of its own. With her dirty blonde hair and unattractive appearance, these characteristics formed a mixture that the locals referred to as 'freak' and 'macabre'. Eventually Macabre became her nickname and she grew up mostly alone without any support or guidance from her mother who was too consumed by alcohol to pay attention. Martha never knew her father; supposedly he died when she was 3. Although she was a total outsider and recluse, she became a wildly passionate romantic. She would spend hours dreaming of being married to a handsome gentleman and having children of their own. But no one would give Martha a second look. Buried in isolation, she began to pursue any understandable knowledge of the dark arts. She loved the night and all the horrible creatures that she had heard about as a child, which flourished her imagination. When she was 10 she witnessed a play entitled 'Frankenstein' and it left her spellbound. When she turned 17 she went to

22

"Ma Cobb"

the fair to go see the haunted house attraction that the poster had mentioned. She bought a ticket and stood in line to enter the horror-filled show. As she was there she noticed a young man staring back at her. He had oily mid length hair, a long forehead, and a scraggly unshaven face yet Martha found him oddly attractive. He came up and introduced himself as Byron and offered to escort her within the terror trip ahead. Shyly, she smiled and nodded in accordance. When they were inside the dark house he stopped her in a corner hidden from the flashing strobe lights and proceeded to touch her all over. She was very nervous and sensed it wrong, the sudden promiscuous actions, but it felt too good for her to resist. There in the darkness she lost her virginity to a complete stranger. After they were finished, he walked on ahead through the haunted maze and when she finally regained her senses and exited the thrill-filled house, she couldn't find her new acquaintance anywhere. Searching all throughout the fairground, she went home with no avail. She cried for weeks but never saw him again.

9 months later she had her first child; a boy that she named Simon. After her pregnancy, the local loser boys saw her as a perfect unwed mother who they could use anyway they wanted. Being poor, insecure and desperately alone, she gave in to their demands and wound up pregnant again. This time she had me. No man ever stayed with her after he got what he wanted. She continued to have relations with men who would run away after she became fertilized. It's like she didn't care anymore. She eventually had 7 children (4 boys, 3 girls) from 7 different fathers, all of whom left long before they had to endure any parental duties or responsibilities.

Martha had acquired the old farmhouse that was her mother's and that is where she raised the children. Only 6 though, because one child, 'Lydia' died only 2 weeks after birth. But she wasn't dead when she was buried. Martha had assumed the baby was dead because she had not cried nor made a sound for one day. Since Lydia had been crying almost nonstop since birth, Martha made the assumption without any official confirmation and then buried her in the backyard. I would've sworn that night I could hear the cries but mother wouldn't let us investigate. About 4 nights later I snuck out and dug up my little sister's box of a coffin and I could tell that she had been moving around after we put her to rest. But it was too late. Quietly I resealed the box and then recovered the grave with the cold wet dirt.

After awhile, dealing with her loneliness and the pressure of singularly raising 6 children, 'Ma Cobb', as she instructed us to call her, had a nervous breakdown which culminated in her losing most of her sanity. She began punishing her offspring without any real motive. It was as if she was blaming us for how her life turned out.

“Ma Cobb”

The farmhouse was old, rundown, very secluded without a neighbor for many miles. The wood was cold with bare insulation and the water would freeze up often. The bathroom was like an indoor outhouse and we all shared blankets but never found much warmth. In the evenings Ma Cobb would drink her coffee, savoring it as if her mug held the last coffee bean to ever come from Columbia. Often we would watch through the cracks as she sat quietly. Knowing that later on she would come to punish us for some deed we may or may not have done. Out back of the house there was a rusty electric fence. It was old and sharp yet still working. Sometimes when she felt we were really naughty she would hold us against it until we yelled all we could yell. Then she would drag us one by one to the musty shed and lock us in there for the night. The cold air would chill to the bone.

As time went on, the acts became more grotesque. We had many varieties of animals on the farm and as a new torture she would strap us down and fling a scared kitty at our faces while we were tied up. The cat’s claws would scratch and tear up our flesh, drawing blood on many occasions. Other times she’d take only one of us, especially my sister Nina and brother Billy, out into the field where she had them perform unspeakable acts to the animals for her sick perverse pleasure. Nina would be forced to lie down, pull up her skirt, take off her panties, and let the dog, horse, or mule sodomize her. Nina would come back crying and bleeding. They would not speak of their torment but we could hear their pleading cries from across the farm.

Finally our eldest brother Simon decided to fight back. One day when mother came to punish Simon he pushed her down and ran out the door, over the electric fence, and into the nearby woods. Mother then tied everyone else up and grabbed a lawn rake and took off after Simon. The night passed and finally she came home and released us. Simon wasn’t with her. We never saw him again. Ma Cobb had stated that she never found him but I saw the rake afterward in the shed. It had dark hardened spots all over it. I am certain it was the color of dried blood. Later that week we were also served with what mother said was a ‘wild animal kill’. The taste was a bit strange yet familiar. My stomach tied in knots to question what it really was. Could it be Simon’s flesh? I didn’t want to know. We all ate because we were nearly starving. Yet deep down, I felt queasy about it.

Months later I also discovered that mother was mixing dog and other animal excrement into our food. I saw her blending it together one day as I peeked through a window in the kitchen. I was disgusted at the sight and wondered if she hadn’t put her own fecal matter in there. She would save her bowel movements though we never understood why. Obviously this

"Ma Cobb"

defecation had to have some use to her. I could no longer eat at the dinner table. I became really weak and skinny. She would call me a limey bastard though she wasn't from England or Europe. I guess she just liked the phrase. I taught myself to read and secretly read old books and newspapers lying around in the attic. Mother never caught me but she knew I was becoming comprehensible.

One day, Elizabeth and Andy, the middle children, decided that they weren't doing any more chores. When Ma Cobb came to assign duties, Andy and Liz pretended to not hear her and ignored her wishes. She slapped them hard but they still refused. Mother grabbed them both and took them to the freezer box where she stored a large quantity of frozen meat for the winter. Opening the door like a coffin, she dumped both the screaming siblings inside. Then she locked it shut so they couldn't escape. I pleaded with her to release them but she threw the rest of us, Nina, Billy, and myself, in the shed. The next day after promising to behave, Ma let us out to go do our chores.

I then plotted my escape from this terrifying nightmare of a life. I tried to convince my brother, Billy, and sister, Nina, but they refused to comply, perhaps too fearful of the consequences. I waited for the prefect moment to make my getaway. Knowing that I could never just walk out undetected, I had to create a diversion. Ma Cobb was sitting in her old worn out rocking chair having her evening coffee in silence. Quietly I walked toward her equipped with my baseball bat, ready to inflict damage. I knew, however, that I had to position my plastic toy just right. When I was just a few feet away from mother I stopped. With my bat clinched tight, I held my breath and said in a low voice 'Ma Cobb'. Startled, she put her coffee cup and saucer on a nearby table and mumbled, 'What? What do you want, you limey bastard?' 'I was just wondering if I may go outside and play ball,' I replied. 'No, not now, I'm busy. I can't be there to keep an eye on you, too.' 'But Ma!' I pleaded. 'Run along now Vlan,' she imperatively suggested as she reached for another sip of scalding hot coffee. As she pressed the faded blue cup against her lips, I swung my toy bat as hard as I could. It connected with a thundering sound and the scalding coffee came spewing out in the desired direction: in mother's face. She screamed in pain as she fell on her knees to the floor. I then ran toward the front door. As I turned the knob, I felt a sudden pang as I looked down to see the saucer for her coffee flying with velocity and connecting with my left leg as it shattered on impact. The throbbing pain was immense but I undauntingly kept running. Out of the house and over the fence I jumped, screaming in agony. I ran toward the woods, occasionally looking behind me to see if she was following. I never saw her. While this was comforting, not knowing where she could be was terrifying. I just continued running, with a limp, and taking as few breaks as possible. I was in the woods for 5 days until I stumbled on the path where I finally passed out. That's where you found me."

The sheriff's face held a look of terror and disgust with his jaw dropped in awe. "You get some rest, son. I'll go check out the farmhouse," the sheriff said with voice trembling. He got in his police car and headed toward Black Bare. On his way, the sheriff got caught in a nasty thunderstorm. Barely able to see the road, he cautiously drove until he reached the Ma Cobb place. He, armed with flashlight and pistol, opened the door and proceeded to search the area around the house. No one was to be found. Quietly he crept up the porch steps to enter to house. The living room was dusty, messy, and smelled of weeks old garbage. Yet no one seemed present. The sheriff heard a soft noise in the adjacent bedroom. Slowly he opened the musty door and peered inside. Rrrrargh! He slammed his fingers in the door in a reflexive jerk to avoid contact with the solid black dog that was chained in a corner of the room and was now showing teeth and growling very antagonistically. His heartbeat accelerated.

Meanwhile, back at the hospital, the nurse comes in to check the vitals of young Vlandon only to find to her surprise that he is not there. She wondered how he could've left without the monitors alerting the nurses' station. As she turned to leave the room, the nurse noticed that Vlan's roommate had two IV's stuck in his arm.

At the Cobb farm, the rain continues to downpour making seeing far distances nearly impossible. The sheriff inspected every area of the house yet found no one. He did find evidence of torture and sadistic acts. Chains, whips, and duct tape thrown about like dirty laundry. With his flashlight providing little light, he went back out into the flood and continued searching around the perimeter looking for clues. He came to the rusty electric fence and observed what he concluded must be 4 graves. There were 4 tobacco sticks planted way into the ground and each had enough space between the other to hold a body. As he stood there inspecting the graves, a jolt came when he was suddenly involuntary lunged onto the fence. In a state of shock, the sheriff fought against his attacker to escape the hazardous position he was in. After having no luck reaching the opponent with his limbs, he forced himself upward and came hard with a head butt to gain freedom. Turning around, the sheriff grabbed his pistol and began firing off the chambers. Through the heavy rain he could see the old woman before him. She was holding a post with some rusted barbed wire wrapped around it. One end had been whittled into a sharp point. As she stood there gasping from the gunshot wounds, she gave a sudden thrust of the post right into the chest of the sheriff. They both fell to the ground.

"Ma Cobb"

As the sheriff lies there mortally wounded, he sees the remaining children gather around him. He pleads for them to help him when Vlandon shockingly appears before him. With breath still inside him, he watches helplessly as all the children collect sharp objects and begin to tear open his flesh. They squirm their dirty hands inside him and take out his inner tissue and organs. They all commence feasting. When they finish with the now deceased sheriff, they all gather around their mother. Each is soaked with human blood and excretions. Ma Cobb looks up with a happy grin and says, "That's my offspring". The children lean toward her with a loving glance and quietly dig their fingernails and sticks into her wrinkled skin. Ma Cobb releases one last shrieking scream as Vlandon tears open her chest and begins eating her heart. Then the other two join him in the consumption. Days later, police officers searched the area but found no clues as to there whereabouts of the missing sheriff and Ma Cobb family.

- - - END

23

"The Murder Gene"

In 2083 an American scientist and genetic researcher named Jasper O' Hanna discovered the ability to find and isolate the murder gene. Everyone who will become a killer in the future has the DNA impression at birth imprinted in a tiny lobe of the cerebellum. Every test conducted has verified the results to be fact. Now with this new knowledge and technological breakthroughs, police officials are able to weed out these destructors beforehand; thus preventing many future disasters that would otherwise inevitably occur. Every newborn now gets a mandatory screening to determine if they are to be potential threats. Those who are "M" positive are then taken away from their biological parents and put under strict government observation. With the advancement of a testing facility in every major city nationwide, every American citizen is sent a summons to be individually tested. The test is masked as a preventive from outbreak. Therefore the public is not fully aware of the procedures.

Zane is an intern at the Genetic Clinic located in Indianapolis, Indiana. He loves just slacking around, doing as little as possible. Some days he is carrying reports while other days he's cleaning the John. When he gets off work he goes to hang with his best friend of 7 years, Sonny. Sonny was the 2083 version of a hippie or beatnik. Very peaceful, loving, creative, non-aggressive. Together they were a dynamite pair, a mischievous yet playful laugh riot. Both being completely intrigued with time travel, they found it to be their hobby and passion. Sonny was jumping up and down waving a card in front of Zane. "Hey man, I have been summoned," Sonny proclaimed. "By what, a town trolley?" Zane apathized. "No man, by the Untied States of America to be screened for any possible rare medical diseases at the Genetic Clinic on Miller Drive. "Holy shit, dude" Zane said. "I get to see your ass get screened tomorrow." "Uh huh" Sonny replied. "And you know I'll be taken captive for I am one murdering son-of-a-bitch." "Yep, you sure are. No doubt about it," Zane sarcastically stated. Sonny wasn't worried about the test. He knew the rare disease screen meant the "are you a murderer" screen. He was indeed very confident that he wasn't going to kill anyone. Hell, he didn't even have any enemies that he knew of.

The next day Sonny went to the clinic and sat impatiently in the waiting room until being called in. He then sat down and after a few tests, went to the table and lied down in front of a huge machine that was before him. He closed his eyes as the doctor slid the front of the device over Sonny's head, awkwardly clamping onto the skin. After about 20 minutes of various scans, he was done with the procedure. The doctors informed him that results would take about a week. One last fill out form and he was done. Later on Sonny went to Zane's place to hang out. Zane said he heard a

"The Murder Gene"

rumor about an old wise hermit who had the knowledge and equipment to alter time. Sonny laughed, nodded, and dismissed the story. Days go by and Sonny forgot all about the screening. Six days after Sonny's tests were performed, Zane was on duty at the clinic. Tonight he was taking samples to the filing office. Often he worked late hours and there were few people still at work. When no one was looking, he unlocked the door to the main office where all the confidential files were kept. He had stolen and cloned a key to get in, for he wasn't authorized. Some nights Zane would sneak in to hide from his supervisor or he'd come in to look up test reports on random people he knew. Tonight he was looking for the list on new inductees into the murder gene hall of fame to see if he knew any of them. As he scrolled down the list he came to something that made his jaw drop and his heart seemingly stop. Sonny's name was on the list. He pulled up Sonny's file to be sure. Same full name. Same address. This brought a panic over Zane. He stood there frozen. He pretended to be sick in order to leave work early and then he rushed over to Sonny's house to inform him of this shocking crisis. When Zane got to Sonny's place, he found his pal sleeping. With a loud yell, Zane awoke Sonny who jumped in startled confusion. After being explained the situation, Sonny sat looking with a frozen glare. He couldn't believe this was happening. He's completely non-aggro, a pacifist to the end. Could the test be wrong? It's accepted as fact. All the rumors about those who are "ill" with this gene ran through his mind. Quarantines, lobotomies, put to death. Total loss of freedom. Every inch of him wanted to run away. But to where? The security teams would track him down easily. Had to be another way. He dreamed of a quick silent escape. "Wish I could time travel," Sonny exclaimed. Zane began to brainstorm. "Shit dude," Zane said. "Let's go find that old hermit fucker and see if he's for real." Sonny thought the hermit's reputation was bogus but he didn't really have any options. They went to the Circle Mall to find a guy who supposedly had directions to the hermit's hideaway. They drove eight miles out of the city and into a rural area shrouded in forest and wilderness. They found the road where the directions said to turn left on. The road came to a dead end. From there they hiked up steep hills to the entrance of a cave. Sonny had well equipped his comrade and himself with flashlights and glow-sticks. They investigated the dark tunnel entrance. They gradually made their way through the beginning and continued to look for any sign of life. About ten minutes into the cave they were getting anxious yet they kept persistent. Sonny shined the light on the cavern walls and froze in horror. Along the sides were bones of various animals and dark stains along the wall. The guys looked at each other knowing someone or something was nearby. Five minutes later they ventured forward and found the old hermit man who was meditating in perfect stillness. "Excuse me," Zane injected, "are you the wise master of time travel?" the old man broke his trance, gazed up at the trespassers and said, "huh?" "Well, w-w-we heard that you can alter time" Sonny explained. The primitive looking and ragged man sat silent for minutes as if in deep thought. Then he began his interrogation. "Why are you seeking to be meddling in these waters? Who are ya running from? Criminals, are ya? Just wanting to escape your present life? Life can be trying. Boring at best. Seems more exciting in another era, eh? Well, it's the same as it always was. The way it's always been. Nothing's changed. Same hardship as in any other time. Surviving is the grand obstacle. All you really have to do is die. That's the one common trait of everything." Sonny peered downward and started to explain his plight. "So you see sir, I just need to get away from here. Too much oppression. Too many accusatory implications. Help me if you can." There must have been something about the desperation in Sonny's voice that clicked with the old man's empathic side. He agreed to show Sonny how. The guys came to learn that the hermit had once been a brilliant chemist but he had ideas that were too radical for modern scientists to accept. Shortly thereafter, He was fired from his position. Before he was terminated, he found the formula for time travel. Mixing the right compounds, elements, and ions, he found a way to create a small wormhole into the surrounding atmosphere. When he left the facility, he took many of the necessary ingredients with him as a personal consolation severance package. Yet he still needed Plutonium and Sulfuric Oxide. He instructed the boys to sneak into the college lab and steal their supply. Then they would need a colder climate. The three of them set out to climb the highest hill around the region to perform the ritual. By this time officials back home in Indiana were already inquiring of Sonny's whereabouts to friends and family members. Finally reaching the top of the nearest towering landscape, Sonny peered over the small towns and distant city lights that seemed all connected from this distance. The effect of the wormhole directly depended on the concoction in which establishes the date. The amount of Carbon would determine how far back in time the warp would be. No specific accuracies but close enough. Sonny had decided to go back one year before his birth to see if he could alter things. He wanted the change his past somehow. The old genius knew precisely how much Carbon intake it would require. With the right formula set, the old man conjures the air around to transform into a surreal hot spot. Sonny, deep in desperation, gives a strong look to Zane and, in another

"The Murder Gene"

minute, disappeared into the bizarre portal.

Ending #1: Sonny goes back in time a year before his birth to stop his parents from ever getting together. He ends up distracting them until they never meet each other. As they find others mates, he vanishes from never being born.

Ending # 2: Sonny goes back in time a year before his birth to stop his parents from ever getting together. He kept trying to divide them but to no avail. They get together and they consummate their love. Thus, Sonny still lives and the police from 2083 have tracked him back in time and force him into a corner where he finally commits suicide thus becoming a murderer.

Ending #3: He, in trying to segregate his parents, ends up being attracted to his much younger and hipper mother. They eventually sleep together (she unaware of who he is). Together they have a deformed offspring version of himself. The child still gets arrested with the gene.

Ending #4: Sonny and Zane both go back in time and decide to stay in limbo, never going back to current time.

Ending #5: Sonny goes back in time a year before his birth to stop his parents from ever getting together. He tries to divide them but found that it's harder that he thought. He eventually kills his mom to stop the cycle from ever happening. He then vanishes.

Ending #6: Sonny goes back in time a year before his birth to stop his parents from ever getting together. He stops his parents from being lovers but she falls for another guy and becomes pregnant. Sonny returns home to find himself altered and a half brother to his best friend Zane.

Ending #7: The warp is a hoax. The authorities come and take Sonny away where he can be under observation. He dies in a padded cell.

Ending #8: Everyone who is held captive with the gene breaks free and starts killing those who locked them away. Proving that everything is predestined.

Epilogue: A year and a half later the government has annulled and discontinued the murder gene theory. Apparently the information was faulty.

24

"**The Nocturnal** (forbidden blood)"

Darkness. It never gets called that anymore. The sun rarely shines in this dim city. The smog is a permanent fixture. The clouds came and settled in with the creatures. They ravage the streets in the late hours, torturing any humans they find. I know because I was one of those humans. I'll get to that soon, but first, a little backstory: Vampires, the undead, nosferatu, nocturnals, or whatever you prefer, are the monsters that inhabit every dark alleyway and old abandoned building in the city. The townspeople are terrified. Unlike ancient folklore and mythology, the real vampires are not immortal. They do however survive much longer than the average human. Human blood is their main dietary supplement, but they can eat or drink anything. Their strength is far greater than any living being. Vampires can survive as long as two or three centuries before drying out. Their insides slowly rot and wither up until there is nothing left. The raisin-like effect. Outside they appear unchanged, while inside they become a hollow shell. The nosferatus are impervious to garlic, crosses, and wooden stakes through the heart. While they do not like the sunlight, it is not destructive to the undeads. They are therefore very difficult to destroy or even wound. This leaves only two ways for a bloodsucker to meet its doom: the withering of time or an injection of menstrual blood. Vampires feed off regular blood to survive but coming in contact with a woman's blood from her period makes the satan spawn completely regress until there is nothing left but ash. The blood associated with birth will fatally wound the night creatures.

A few rouge vigilantes try to bait the vampires and using a supply of this sacred blood, luring them to their final death. My brother Cade was one such warrior. One night I was walking home from work, Cade was playing guardian as usual. Everything was a little too quiet. We were suddenly attacked by three hungry vampires, two plain males and a female bearing a wide assortment of jewelry and ornaments. The two males grabbed my brother while the female dealt with me. She was too strong to overpower and with little effort, had me pinned down behind a trash receptacle in a desolate alleyway. With the streetlight's glow, I could make out the shadow of my brother and his perpetrators on the wall of the adjacent building. As she held me down, I watched in horror as, with a wince of pain, Cade was torn apart limb by limb and then devoured as tonight's main course. I closed my eyes and waited for my similar fate. It never came. The two flunkies disappeared off into the night. The female vampire held me with one hand and began undressing me with the other. I struggled frantically but it was no use. Eventually I was naked on the concrete and gagged with my own panties. She began running her fingers across my clit. I cried for mercy but she was unrelenting. After awhile she ran her finger inside of me. Then fingers. Then her fist. It hurt so bad I thought I was going to pass out or vomit. She pulled out and slowly inserted another object inside me. It was cold and slightly prickling. I wasn't foreign to this tool though, just never had someone else do it to me. She began trusting it in and out. The horror was a slow motion nightmare that seemed to never end. When a man rapes a woman, he stops after he cums but when a woman rapes, she can go on forever. She repeated all of her tortures and lied on top of me, piercing my flesh with her erect nipples. She sucked my skin and bit my tit until it bled. She began licking her hands that were covered in blood from the hardcore fisting she had done. Looking at me in a weird seductive way, she tasted the dark liquid. Then a light bulb went off in my head! I had just started my period earlier that day. Just hadn't got to my supplies to protect myself yet, it happens. I'm sure my blood mixed with the forced blood she created. I was sure she would disintegrate and determined to watch her die when I passed out from blood loss.

I came to in the middle of the day, covered in a ragged old blanket and lying beside the trash bin. As I slowly regained my senses, I stumbled around the area as the events of the previous night began to slide show in my head. As I saw the replay of my brother's death, a sharp pain arose in my chest. I limped and staggered until I reached home. Upon entering the door, I fell on the floor and crawled toward my bathroom. Throwing off the stinking blanket, I flung myself into the bathtub and ran warm water all over my body. I sat there washing all the dried blood off me and wishing I had seen the final moments of the bitch vampire before she evaporated into thin air. Bitch got what she deserved. I decided that after I healed I would carry on the mission that Cade died so honorably for. After a few days though, I noticed some strange changes happening to me. First, my period did not run its cycle. In fact it stopped after that night. Then I began staying up late in the deep nocturnal hours, finding that I was more alert then. Weird cravings came over me. It was obvious what was happening to me. I was pregnant! Little shit swore he always used a condom. Lying fucker. Maybe that's not it. Could just be sick with the flu or something. I saw my doctor and had extensive tests ran but all results were negative and nothing was found except a slow heartbeat rate. I walked around in the early morning hours and it became unavoidably clear: I was turning into one of them. Slowly but surely, my fate had been sealed. I decided to take out as many of them as I could before I fell victim. The plan was to avenge my brother and destroy his killers. Using a supply of menstrual blood bought from a second hand peddler on Brooke Lynn Street, I waited patiently for any sign of the creatures. Finally, I got a nibble playing the bait. I slowly turned back to see a pair of vamps sneaking toward me. With my jar of purifying blood attached to my belt, I dipped the blade of my dagger into the liquid and then turned around to attack. They were right upon me but I was fast enough to maneuver myself around to get a good stab into the flesh of one. I was awestruck as I saw for the first time the effects that a woman's blood could have on these demons. The other vamp made a gash in my skin but luckily I had time to re-dip and slice this piece of shit in two, as well. I stood there catching my breath and feeling well accomplished for my first night of undead slaying. But the night was still young. I searched old alleys hoping to find the scum who took away my brother. Before I knew it I came to an old unused warehouse that had been boarded up. Walking past the deserted building, I heard a noise coming from inside. Stepping up on a broken air conditioner, I cautiously peered into the dusty window of the warehouse. There was a gang of vampires inside, all feeding off of one helpless victim. They were gathered around, all taking turns. As the crowd shifted, my eyes looked with total disbelief. There stood the nocturnal girl who raped and turned me. How could it be? She tasted the blood between my legs. She should be ash, like all the rest. I waited for the perfect opportunity to strike. After awhile many of the vamps cleared out of the building. When the ratio became somewhat reasonable I made my move. Breaking the glass with my dagger's handle, I brushed away the debris and jumped into the warehouse. All eyes were immediately on me. I gutted a couple as I made my way toward the target. Soon there was a circle of blood hungry fiends around me. As they started closing in, I gripped my blade and prepared to swing. Then the female yelled in a commanding voice "**stop**". She glided toward me and touched my chin with her hand. She looked down at my jar of blood and smiled. Before I knew what was happening, she came at me with a blow to the face and wham! I was out.

When I came to, I was stripped to my undergarments and chained to a wall in what was a beautiful room of ancient architecture with vast amounts of gold plated shrines. After an hour or so, the elusive female vampire appeared. She was even more royalty looking than before. "Who and what are you" I asked. "And why aren't you dead"? She drew close to me and sat down in a nearby throne like chair. From there she began to reveal to me her origins: **I am Princess Amra, ruler of all local vampire cliques and beyond. I am the only known nocturnal that is invulnerable to the blood from a woman. Therefore I possess a quality that the others so desperately yearn to have. They see me as the next step in evolution.**

"The Nocturnal (forbidden blood)"

They worship me as a goddess. This, however, was not always the case. I was born a strange hybrid breed between a vampire and a human. My mother was human yet somehow able to carry and give birth to a nocturnal child. Overcome with the shame brought on by fellow humans, my mother eventually took her own life. I was two at the time. I didn't understand why mommy was so still. When they found us, I was licking her blood from the puddle on the floor. I then lived with my father who taught me the ways of the night. We were a poor class of nocturnal and as I grew up the angst of youth overran me. For years I took many boyfriends, yet they never seemed to satisfy me. Eventually I took to enjoying the company of other women exclusively. I was warned early on about the dangers of being with a human female since she has the power to destroy. But being young and naïve, you feel indestructible and you take your chances. I was always drawn to women. Don't get me wrong, I still have the occasional male to snack on but generally I prefer girls. I can remember when I first tasted the forbidden blood. A simple accident. I was drunk off the blood of a sexy young virgin whom I had been toying with for many weeks. The good ones you want to savor. She had the grayest eyes I had ever seen. Such a beautiful body. I was sucking on her inner thigh and in the heat of the moment I got lost in the passion. I began to vigorously lap up her wet and succulent pussy. Unknown to me was the dripping crimson fluid falling from her crotch onto the bed. When I came up for air I got a glimpse of the blood running down my chin. I froze in sudden panic. We are taught that if we have contact with the blood, we crumble into ash. I waited for my end to come. It never did. Somehow, I was immune to the poison. Soon I became notorious and renown for my special ability. Secretly all the nocturnals envied my power yet too fearful to take the chance themselves. I would suck dry the crimson crevice on heavy flow days but no other known vamp could do the same. I sired the girl who I first drank and we became heated lovers. I think she loved me furiously. When we had a guest, if it was that time of the month she would always try to taste it. I would always deny her access to the womanly area for fear of losing her life. I wanted to save her all for myself. But she was reluctant. One night without my guidance she brought a woman home and chained her up. The woman wasn't on her period so my love hid the prisoner from me. Then when the blood came, she gathered the strength and licked it up. In mere minutes she was a pile of ash on the floor. Days later,

"The Nocturnal (forbidden blood)"

I found my lover's remains and the woman hostage. She informed me what happened. I was devastated. Lonely. Full of rage. I went a little mad for a while and began my reign of terror on anyone I came in contact with. I sucked and fucked and left them dying. Eventually I gathered my senses. Then I began my quest to find myself another mate. Now I think I may have found her replacement. Her lips were so close to my face I could feel the cold breath. I didn't know how to respond. I wanted to spit in her face. But I knew I had to play it cool. I pretended that I was warming up to the idea of being her sex slave, hoping that would inevitably lead to my freedom from bondage. It took a month. A month of hearing her autobiographical stories and letting her kiss me wherever she liked. She would enter the room covered in human blood and feed me with her tongue. I almost gagged every time yet I stomached it. Finally I was released and sent to her quarters. When I entered the room, she was naked lying spread on the bed. She motioned me to her and began to undress me. Licking and sucking my every pore, she inserted her fingers inside of me. I gave out a bittersweet moan. We had sex for hours. It was a forced situation yet a passionate pleasure all the same. In the near dawning hours, we are entangled in an embrace, fulfilled from the previous workout. I awoke in a panic. Quietly, I got out of her clutches and stood over the bed. I wanted to kill her then and there. But I didn't know how. So instead I gathered my clothes and silently fled the room. As I was leaving I spotted two vamps guarding the doorway to the exit. I took a double take and I was sure they were the bastards who murdered Cade. Reaching in my pants back pocket where my blade was, I whistled in a sexy way to get their attention. They started to salivate immediately. As they drew closer, I, with one lightning speed swing, slashed both their throats. I had no fresh supply of menstrual blood but there was a vast amount of dried blood covering the blade. Which apparently works just as well. They were dust. I spilt.

It's been years now since I saw her last. I hear stories of her from time to time. Some urban legends, some definitely true. In ways, I hate her because she cursed me. In ways, I should thank her for giving me a new life. She was one high and mighty, crazy as shit, sexy and powerful bitch. Nowadays I survive on what she taught me. Because now I am all nocturnal.

(End credits as the main character comes up for air with blood all over her face.)   END.

" Zeitgeist "

~~~Intro – black screen – music plays as credits roll ~~~
~~~Song: Bad Religion's "A World Without Melody" ~~~

"I don't want to live in a world without melody / Sometimes the rhythmic din of society is too much for me / But purpose is prioritized these days, the goal is win the prize / There's a sleeping resonance we hold, through which we are unified / So let it out! Don't just be one in the crowd / Hesitance and diffidence will do you in / And your soul doesn't care for social medicine / And I've got this hunch about you and me / none of us are ready for a world without melody / Melody is the key / It's the surest way to unlock your individuality / Melody is the key / It will set you free! / And I know together we could change the world / Just you and me / But I won't live without melody..."

~~~song abruptly stops. Black screen with silence. ~~~

Marion Narrating: They say that everything ends eventually. Seems that's true. Some, however, believe that with enough time and space things can begin again. And these new beginnings were what I yearned for. I've heard that life used to be so different. The total fabrication of society has been drastically altered since the so-called "Entertainment Age". A few years after the last millennium things started to change. The finely tuned machine of culturalized civilization began to crumble. At least those who operated under the influence of the western ways. Primitive cultures remained pretty much the same I guess. After many years of suppression and control, the citizens began to revolt in a new passive way. They didn't fight with protests, guns, or wars. They fought with silence and apathy. Turned their backs on the traditions and customs. All the subliminal control substances were discarded. All the mass products weren't bought or consumed. Forcing mega corporations to go out of business. Many formed merges and consolidations that in time diminished as well. The news media, with their constant illustrations of terror and fear, were ignored and forgotten. All these events caused a backlash of massive job lay offs.

One of the main aspects of the entire culmination was the collapse of the entertainment industry. All the music, movies, literature, video games, paintings, as well as any other form of art were abandoned. The first reason for this was that the individuals began feeling too manipulated by these commercialized industries. The second and main reason was that with all the new technology with affordable prices, everyone would have the same advantage at making these forms of media. In other words, the average Joe
~~~

" Zeitgeist "

sitting at home could make a record that sounded just as good as the four or five million dollar deals made with the major corporations. This caused way too many accessible choices to ever decide on what is "now the next popular thing". Same way with movies, books, etc… everyone was getting their own fifteen minutes and all the "talented" became a blur by so many talented yet otherwise unheard of acts. The stars were no longer stars. Just mere mortals with no more ability than you could do yourself. So everyone kind of evened out on the popularity scale. No more gods to worship. The aftershock hit like a ton of bricks. So with a great sounding full potential band next door, a creative filmmaker across the street, and a gifted writer down the block, everything became too accessible. Too easy. The markets of media all crashed. Basically what happened was overkill. There came a breaking point where it seemed that everyone had a massive surplus of entertainment. Enough that they couldn't enjoy them all. Everyone and their mother owned way too many CDs, DVDs, books, etc…. With the internet file sharing programs, people had everything they wanted. The problem was that after they got it, they didn't want it. Millions of people had more music, films, and other art forms than their children's children could ever use. Finally it happened. They all individually and then collectively gave up these "real life distracters" and forfeited their use to their lives. The value dropped to zero. After so many years every musical chord had been used over and over. Every story told time and time again. Everything became so remade and rehashed that no one wanted to do it anymore. "All the greats have been done," they would say. So what do you do when everything under the sun has been done? Nothing. That's what they did. After the failure of the amalgamations and overabundances, no one delved into the artistic domains and therefore negated any new material to be created. Entertainment became a taboo that no one would shame themselves to partake in. So those forms of expression and communication vanished. Many other stipulations were abandoned or inverted. With the cultural expression in stalemate, people began to rely on word of mouth and other means to connect, while any thought of venting creatively was suppressed and forgotten.

The major change that occurred was that no one any longer acknowledged a god or religion. Organized religion was dismissed as another form of manipulation and mind control. The churches were abandoned. Bibles were burned or put away. The time scale changed. The new ideas proposed the extinction of the B.C., A. D. time line. Now no dates exist. Anything before today is referred to as "before". Specific

" Zeitgeist "

times and dates became unimportant. "What's past is past," was the coined phrase often heard.

Many other adjustments were made as well. The government was still intact but not with a singular ruler. People no longer relied on campaigns to win elections. The officials were selected electronically. Computers were still useful to the new world, just not to create things. Health care became available and free to all. No one had to go in debt from a death in the family as insurance companies were seen as vile profit organizations that made a fortune off another's tragedy. Every road became an interstate of sorts to make traffic safer for everyone.

The people began to loathe synthetic beauty as well. Therefore many cosmetic products were left unused by the would-be consumers. Plastic surgeons had no patients. Bras became an idle fashion norm because the people felt that they offered unrealistic enhancements to serve as sex appeal. The whole sex sells gimmick was over.

Humans were getting back to the root of all their evils and nipping the buds. Purifying the world from the corruption that has long zombified the weaker ones and made them all consuming animatrons who work to buy unneeded products to fill a hollow void inside which cannot really be filled with anything. Therefore they constantly must feed the hunger inside. Thus repeating the cycle so everything falls into place.

But as everything ends, eventually it did. At least all of this is what my grandfather tells me. See I was born into this barren age. Now the world is a desolate unimaginative land of hard truths. I'm told it is better now in many ways. There is no Santa Claus or Easter bunny, whatever that is. Nothing here really but working for survival until death. Medicine is still used but now given freely to those in need. The average life span has drastically increased for both sexes. Harmful products such as tobacco, alcohol, and illegal drugs have become a rare commodity. Many people want to live as long as they can because they are taught from an early age that death is coming and nothing follows it. So with the fake world stripped away, reality became a constant reminder that life is depleting always. The object of society isn't to gain higher power but to help expand the threshold for everyone. All of this may sound like a great utopia but believe me, it wasn't. The emptiness I felt inside was slowly but surely developing into a fierce burning eating me alive. I felt incomplete. I knew something was missing, I just didn't know what. I was determined to find my cure.

My name is Marion Michaels, just a guy trying to find his way in the world. And while scene groups have all disappeared, it's still common to assemble with those who share common attributes. These are my people:

" Zeitgeist "

Zeke is a completely cool yet insane cosmic drama Zen master. In other words, he is funny and full of shit at the same time. He swears his great great grandfather had the ingenious idea to patent the renting of musical CDs just like VHS tapes. Until the internet file sharing programs ruined it for him. He then went mad and did nothing productive. Cilia is a prime example of a gothic girl. The whole goth look has faded out but Cilia has all the inner turmoil and darkness to fit the bill. She doesn't dress in black with spikes and chains. As a matter of fact, her hair isn't black or dyed at all; it is light brown. But her thoughts cling to death and other weird observations that earn her the title. Len is a little paranoid. Ok, a lot paranoid. She will not drink from cans or eat out of most containers for fear of some contamination. Or even worse, fear of someone doing sick things to them. She lives in constant alert to not fall under the control of "them". Calorie and gas mileage counter all the way. Kurdt is a nihilist with perfect hair who doesn't care for much except maybe his hair. He eats cereal and chugs milk with it because he says it has the same effect as the "normal" way. He's constantly inventing things; only to find someone else beat him to it. He believes that most knowledge is trivial and that it only gains importance by the individual who cares or cares not for it. In other words, what's meaningful to one is completely meaningless to another. Value depends on the person. Last in our little clique but certainty not least is Sonia. She's the perfect human specimen in my eyes. Blonde, bright, beautiful in every way. If love existed, I swear I'd love this girl. My only problem is…well… I've never told her how she attracts me. Every time I try, I fall limp, word wise anyway. So until I can muster up the courage, I will keep this a secret and continue as her friend while she remains oblivious.

Marion: "How goes it guys?"

~~~ Cilia snarls nose ~~~

Cilia: "Aaaaaaahh"

Zeke: "Dude, my aura is a frustrated flux of colors."

Marion: "Know the feeling. I've been in this funk for a while. Can't shake it."

Kurdt: " I went down to the waterfall today. Sat on the big rocks and just looked up at the sky. Felt kind of numb but it's better than like shit I guess."

Len: "I'm so bored. But what else is new?"

Marion: "Sorry guys. Too many tales from 'before'. Got you guys as inquisitive as I am. Longing for something I never knew. How fucked up is that? Anyway… What's we doing tonight?"
~~~

" Zeitgeist "

Cilia: *'How about going into the city and listening to all the new opportunities the officials have announced? Huh, what's say?"*
Marion: "Oh yeah sounds good. Or perhaps for better fun, we could take shards of glass and ram them into our eye sockets."
~~~everyone smiles and laughs ~~~
Zeke: "Let's all go meditate near the rock quarry. Enjoy the warm night air."
Sonia: "Okay. Then let's go hear some more stories of 'before."
Marion: I dunno. The more I hear, the more I want to live in that era. I know we have advanced toward a purer form of acceptance but damn, how boring it is. I'd like to feel something new. A little spark of hope. Fuck, even if it's fake; anything would be better than this."
Sonia: "Anything? Don't be so sure, Marion. There was a good reason why everyone left behind the corrupt world that came 'before'. While at the same time, we acknowledge the rational side to apply logic; we now embrace our animal side and realize that we aren't any better than the other species. Do you want to think yourself special?"
Marion: "No, you're right. It's just…umm…I dunno…a passion inside me to vent my emotions out into something artistic."
Kurdt: "Man, let it go already."
Marion Narrating: Emotions weren't exempt from change either. Most were stripped to their real value instead of the fake version. Love was instead known as chemical reactions, desire, and need of accompaniment. Therefore, love wasn't considered a true emotion. Anyone in love was delusional. People paired themselves together with the knowledge that the attraction was merely chemical. They also saw the coupling act as a means to simplify life's burdens. Those who didn't believe in this concept simply went from partner to partner without being branded with a stigmatism. The reasons why certain people are compatible still remain a mystery. This was my dilemma with Sonia. Definitely the cutest girl I had even seen. Every time I'm near her, my hands clam up and I just can't be myself. I feel too inferior. She gets to me in a way no one ever has. The girls of before were nothing of her caliber. But I can never muster enough courage and confidence up to ask her to be my mate. But maybe someday…
~~~the group goes to the quarry for some relaxation. Then afterward it's off to see Marion's grandfather for another intriguing night of story telling around a fire. ~~~
Marion Narrating: my grandfather was somewhat a rebel within the new community. It's true he gave up his rights to the old ways but it wasn't all by choice. When the revolution began, it seemed like a

" Zeitgeist "

righteous cause to join. While my grandfather was feeling overwhelmingly oppressed by the system, he didn't necessarily share the need to destroy everything and begin again anew. But when the majority came in favor, those against had to comply with certain changes. That's what happened with him. So when the time came, my grandfather gave up his possessions yet he held a grudge toward the new lawmakers. While it wasn't illegal to have the old materialistic things, most agreed it best to vanish them in order to build a better future. Most adults and elders do not speak of the past ways much. They feel that people could easily regress to the means of manipulation. Yet my grandfather speaks freely of it and tells us tales of fantasy and tragedy. They are terrifying and exciting. But that was my pops. Definitely a true individual.

Marion's Grandfather: "Children! Oh my, such wonderful young faces. Fresh and molding with tender times. Come and sit with me beside the fire."

~~~ Marion kisses his grandfather on the forehead ~~~

Marion: "Hey pops, I've had a beautifully unproductive day. Doing nothing is what I do best. We've all come to hear some more stories of before."

Len: "Yes, please share those enigmatic journeys. They warp my fragile little mind in a good way."

Marion's Grandfather: "Warp you say? Hmmm…maybe I shouldn't be telling all of you those old meanderings."

Zeke: "No, no please do. We need to hear them. Do you realize how boring this planet is? The way you tell it, once shit was happening. Sure bad karma but also good karma. Better than this barren desert of suburbia."

Cilia: "Yep, I think the pain of oppression would be better than the pain of this destitute lifestyle."

Marion: "Exactly what I've been saying all along."

Marion's Grandfather: "Ok children, let's see…once upon a time the new world of the west was an uptight conservative melting pot. The FCC and all their affiliations began putting rating systems on all forms of entertainment. Stickers, warning labels, editing, and content description were all dispersed throughout the land. This was to prevent young influential minds from getting their hands on explicit and radical material. The plan really just backfired. The labels lead these angst hungry youths straight to the wild thought provoking material that the 'powers that be' tried to shelter them from in the first place. Just look for the warning label and you'd find what you were looking for. Ha ha ha."

Kurdt: "That's some funny shit, man. Funny shit."

Cilia: "Pretty wicked. Now tell us again about the religious factions."
~~~

" Zeitgeist "

Len: "oh yes!"

Marion's Grandfather: "Ok, well for hundreds of years the structure of society was held together by rules and regulated fear. Dictators and monarchs had reign over the peasants until the day the peasants said 'enough.' Before then the fear was spread to control those 'lower beings.' The main dread was the punishment of going to hell in the afterlife. Hell was supposedly a place of fire and torment where all the sinners and lost souls would go after death to be tortured for all eternity. Heaven of course was the opposite. Many versions were…"

Marion: "Wait. So there are these two places for 'souls' in an afterlife. Where are these places located? How did the souls get there? What shape did the souls take?"

Marion's Grandfather: "Yes, that was the problem. Most churches painted an elaborate picture of beautiful scenery and a warm tranquility between all humans and animals. They offered hope and a promise of joining with loved ones after death. Hordes of mankind bought into this for years. After several generations, the species began to evolve somewhat. It became clear to the free thinkers that this 'perfect happiness' was completely incomprehensible. How could one or the essence of one join with loved ones especially since not everyone loved the same. The majority were attracted to different individuals. The whole 'everyone in Heaven looking as humans wearing nice clothes' shtick and image became more and more absurd. A soul, if existed, has no eyes to see, no skin to feel, etc… This kind of acceptance led to the gradual decline of the old beliefs. Another observation was that Lucifer, the fallen angel, wouldn't necessarily succumb and follow God's plan of punishment. Being a rebel against the throne, wouldn't he still show apathy toward the righteous? In other words, a spiteful demon wouldn't torture souls sent to him as punishment for not following God's demands. Wouldn't he promote that kind of behavior? The loopholes of the religious oppression began to show through. That is now ancient history. Everyone swore off religion as an unrewarding false worship. No longer were prayers said or communions met. Anyone who now believes in a higher power simply refers to the sexless entity as 'The Maker.' Most of these people are extreme religious fanatics from before.

Another vast breakdown was the complete abolishment of prejudice, racism, sexism, and all other forms of bigotry. It took many centuries to overcome these deep-rooted obstacles. Most everyone before would hate others for what they were and try to force beliefs on others. In time that all dissipated and people came to accept their differences. Gay, black, straight, white, red, bi, on and on: no stigmatisms were held. Now the world is a melting pot of understanding. But I for one feel like some may erupt one day and explode with hatred toward those around. Time will tell. People still conflict of course but they just control the anger better."

Sonia: "Tell us about…uhmmm…what was it called…pottery…no, no that's not it…oh yes, poetry."

Marion's Grandfather: "Ah, poetry: the language of life. Well, poetry and written material were main sources of knowledge and fiction dispersed throughout the land for many many years. But eventually the people burned the books to aspire for a knowledge that the paper could not contain. Everything had been made, written, and told. No one wanted to go there again. That's why all stationary was destroyed including pencils, pens, and paper. People learn everything from the computer now; that is the only form of education and visible communication."

Kurdt: "What...uh…about those petty jobs man used to perform?"

Len: "Yeah, those sound horrible and really dumb. Repetitive robots."

Marion's Grandfather: "They were. They were. Back then jobs were designed to be efficient and mass market producing. Such commodity. Many factories and companies had employees doing the same routine over and over. Some were complete monotony while others were more of a daily routine kind of chore. Psychology studies eventually found these procedures to have a stunt on the growth patterns in human development. If people experience the same thing over and over with little deviation, true evolution could never fully occur. Afterward, everyone began shifting jobs periodically to expand their brain capacity and gain new knowledge. Without the pressure of overworking and stress in the workplace, employees didn't mind being at work. Now that holidays weren't acknowledged or celebrated, the commercialized demand of profit was over and people could work less for there was little to obtain except the necessities for survival. The competitive products weren't there to aim for any longer. Of course, all those industries collapsed under the fall of mass marketing. That signaled the end of all the various name brands and imitations of items. Back then there were so many options it would take all day just to grocery shop. Now of course we have a singular producer of each individual product. The choices have become somewhat limited but everything is affordable. No more market selling strategy for consumers. Food isn't wasted as it was previously. The daily amount of food disposal from major markets was staggering. Such a waste as many went hungry. Now that has turned for the better. A liberal conservatism."

Zeke: "So isn't life really better now?"

Marion's Grandfather: "Well, yes and no. The peaceful bliss of higher knowledge and advancement has brought a stress free unity in society but

" Zeitgeist "

all of the passion has diminished. Everything's too easy, too complacent. The majority view what came before us as hell on earth. Yet I feel this neutral numbness is almost a dead existence. We live to live, no goals or dreams. Homicides have dwindled away but suicides are at an all time high. Why? Because the need to survive and leave a mark on this world isn't instilled in the younger generations. There is no pressure to fit in but there also isn't any desire to continue forward on a questless quest. Maybe we need that false sense of purpose to establish enough motivation for ourselves. Without it, what reason for all of this?"

Kurdt: "Damn, no such thing as a perfect existence is there?"

Marion: "That would be too easy."

Cilia: "So really the power of choice is good but too many choices can ruin the system. Irony at it's most prolific."

Zeke: "Seems like the loss of importance often happens when an overabundance occurs. Nothing is special."

Marion's Grandfather: "And that's why all these factors went corrupt. After something loses its effect, there is little left but to wither. New generations need new techniques, tales, and technology to call their own. When everything maxed out, there was nothing left to claim. With little focus on the 'old new world' ways, the evolution process really began to happen. At least for a while. Now everything is peaked out it seems where very few developments are made. Nothing left to excite the humans. Without motivation, many people lost the lust for life. Nothing to look forward to. No destination or goal. I fear a massive mental breakdown crisis will occur soon if some change isn't made. But eh, what do I know? Everyone thinks I'm a crazy loon."

Sonia: "We don't. You are straight with us about events that happened 'before'. Others often treat it like some fucking conspiracy. Like if we find out, we are doomed to repeat the past or some shit…"

Marion: "Pops, we feel the oppression everyday weighing down like an invisible burden and we aren't sure how much more of this we can actually take cause…"

Marion's Grandfather: "Now son calm it down. Being overemotional will get you nowhere, kind of like apathy. Sometimes patience is the best route to take. Evolution cannot be forced. And one man cannot be a sole judge of…"

Marion: "Judge? Come on now, I remember what you taught me of judges and justice itself. Complete hypocrisy. Isn't that the truth of it all? No real right or wrong, good guy bad guy thing?"

Marion's Grandfather: "Yes, you are correct. When I was young I realized that there was no true justice. Just biased statements of redemption to regulate the herd with a sense of wrongness avenged. But those chastised were all scapegoats, for some were made examples of while the real threats roamed free. For instance, a pack of cars are all speeding and a cop pulls over the last one and gives them a ticket. They were causalities while the other deviants go unpunished. Here's another, if a boy starts a fight with another boy who doesn't want to fight and both get scolded for it. The victim gets scarred from the whole good guy theory, merely for protecting himself. Such corruption had to end and it did. Well, children that's enough fables for one evening."

~~~the group stands and prepares to leave. Everyone says goodbye and loads into Len's vehicle. As Marion heads to join them, his grandfather calls him back to whisper something to him. ~~~

Marion's Grandfather: "My son, I have always tried to be fair with you. I've never candy coated the harsh truths nor tried to force my opinions onto you. However, if you cannot be content in this near perfect existence then I am your sympathist. What no one else will probably tell you is that there is a place where many of the artifacts and tools of before were collected and stored. They have been hidden from public view but should still be well persevered. Well there are two places actually, possibly more. The substantial portion of these possessions was sent to Antarctica. Secretly sealed in a continent where few would ever go. However, one such area is nearby. There is a small canyon about two days journey past the cedar trees and straight through the hills and valleys to the other side. Now deep within this canyon is a door that is buried. This door leads to a storage room carved out by the people to keep all that they wanted to forget. Who knows why they put it all there? As a safety net in case they were wrong? By sentimentalists who just couldn't destroy precious creations? I'm not sure but it all should still be there. Well preserved. Guitars, brushes, paint, design blueprints, pens, paper, etc…The door is sealed with concrete so no one could just stumble on it. But few young people know it exists. My bet is there are surveillance cameras but no one guarding it. That would be too obvious and suspicious. With some masking tape and welding equipment, a man could get into the room no problem. If everything inside you is telling you to find these tools, then I condone your quest fully. Do what you have to do. Just make sure you are willing to risk the consequences of drastic change. It is time for a new voice. I believe you have the gift. Now go and make me proud."

Marion: "…thank you…"

~~~Marion hugs his grandfather and joins the others.

Later:

Marion lies restless in his bedroom ~~~

" Zeitgeist "

Marion Narrating: What do you do when you are given such a powerful option of choice that you fear the doing of one over the other? Afraid to walk the wrong path. I stared at the ceiling for hours imagining scenarios that could transpire. Would my actions corrupt the world and taint all those around me? Would they result in the freedom of art and the sense of accomplishment that creation brings? Would the people convert with me or brand me an outcast? Would art always have to be the scapegoat for manipulation? Do I have the power and the talent to create in the first place? This could be my beast of burden, my undoing…

~~~ Fade to black. Marion grabs black tape and puts in a nearly full duffle bag. Puts the bag in the backseat next to a welding mask. He then gets in his car, cranks the engine, and begins to drive. ~~~

Marion Narrating: Well, this is it. No turning back now. If I had a destiny this would be it. Sometimes change forms on its own yet other times it has to be forced. I am that change maker. I won't be a hero, just a man trying to silence the inner demons. Who knows? Maybe I'll become vain and shallow, worrying more about appearances than substance. Nah, not very likely. I'm going to use every inch of my imagination. Bring excitement back in an old new way. Bring humor back to a world too stern and politically correct to laugh. Everything will be fresh and new. We will get it right this time. Together we'll create for the purpose of communicating and venting, not for money, fame, or popularity. This time art will be our spirituality. We'll save ourselves. And oh yeah, as for Sonia and I, the future may hold promise. When I get the pen and paper, I'm going to write her the greatest sonnet ever penned. She'll feel my adoration. Then I'll write the first love song because it will be the first to her. I won't use heart, moon, or star metaphors but she'll get the point. I'm her soul mate, her sole mate. Perhaps later on we'll create together in a different kind of way, creating our first child. As I make my way to the canyon I know one truth: the power of expression is the only true freedom we ever have.

~~credits roll as R. E. M.'s "It's The End Of The World As We Know It (And I Feel Fine)" plays.
Then full version of Bad Religion's "A World Without Melody" plays.
~~~ **END.** ~~~

Lyrics

Songs written from November 2002 through February 2004 for various musical projects. Most performed live.

Bounce

Many of these lifetimes clash
All colliding with a crash
Spilling onto those we don't know
Take our time descending far
Never knowing who we are
Leave behind unimpressive show
But I am not about to wait
For their petty sick debates
To feel like I can truly belong
Time that I have killed for you
Away now from the things you do
Never again will you string me along
{chorus} :
I won't be your teething toy
Your plaything
I want nothing now yeah right now
Any damage that's to be done
Has been done
This world has brought me down
I'm down
All of every day goes by
Stuck with torture in my mind
Living with my reoccurring scenes
Now all the friends of yesterday
Packed up, moved out, gone away
I have lost control of my dreams
Every time I talk to you
It's evident that I'm the fool
Cause you would never give me hope
I'll just sit here idled by
Waiting for your turn to cry
Then I can watch as you choke
I won't be your teething toy
Your plaything
I want nothing now yeah right now
Any damage that's to be done
Has been done
This world has brought me down
I'm down
Many of my thoughts they clash
Feels like I'm about to crash
Because I can never decide
Where I want my life to go

Bounce (continued)

How to make me truly grow
You come like a plague to my side
But this time you'll be surprised
There's no gleaming in my eyes
Your words won't faze me now
I have put you in your place
An empty forgotten space
So don't show me that innocent smile
I won't be your teething toy
Your plaything
I want nothing now yeah right now
Any damage that's to be done
Has been done
This world has brought me down
I'm down

you make…
make me bounce…
my feelings bounce…
bounce around…
bounce upside down…
you make me bounce…

And I am not about to wait
For your petty sick debate
To feel like I truly belong
I'll be on the road tonight
Wishing I was taking flight
Knowing there is no right or wrong
I won't be your teething toy
Your plaything
I want nothing now yeah right now
Any damage that's to be done
Has been done
This world has brought me down
I'm down
I won't be your teething toy
Your plaything
I want nothing now yeah right now
Any damage that's to be done
Has been done
This world has brought me down
I'm down

Crowd Comfort

All my days, since my birth
Subject to the ways
Force fed lies, hypnotized
Blending with the greys
Led by chains, strict restraint
Taught how to obey
Pulling reins, they create to slave
A prisoner to the grave
Censor me, condition me
A martyr for their fear
Abandon me, without pity
The outcome comes out clear
Refuse to be their zombie
So I'm breaking out of here
Even if I wanted to
I could never be like you
Forget the comfort of the crowd
I must make a unique sound
Ban my rights, cloud my sight
Shut out my own view
I won't exist, on their list
Won't do what I'm told to
Condoned trap, condemned out
Anti by design
Not programmed, by their sham
I'll use my own mind
Censor me, condition me
A martyr for their fear
Abandon me, without pity
The outcome comes out clear
Refuse to be their zombie
So I'm breaking out of here
Even if I wanted to
I could never be like you
Forget the comfort of the crowd
I must make a unique sound

Cyber Stalking

Yesterday I got an anonymous email
Still I opened and read
Scattered words and phrases vowing love for me
The basics of what it said
Deleted the file, thought nothing more of it
Went in a chat room to chat
Message popped up, I clicked ignore user
But then it popped right back

{chorus}:
Now who is invading
My time and space again
Why can't they leave me be
I don't know you
And don't want to
So stop I.M.ing me

Today I went online to check some sites
Logged in with a different screen name
To my surprise, the same person stalking me
Asking for my age, sex, and name
Said that my profile was so touching and deep
And a rendezvous would be wild
Said "no" would not be taken for an answer
This game wasn't laugh out loud

{chorus}

Now who has all this free time on their hands
To invite themselves in a home
Step into my private life, blatant harass
And will not leave me alone

{chorus}
I don't know you
And don't care to
Don't instant message me
Just leave me be
I am busy
Why can't you fucking see

Deserted in the Desert without Dessert

Look around this wasted town
Memories are all around
The past, the pain, it is never far

Longing for the simple days
Time I didn't feel so strange
Now I'm not, I'm not like you are

Worries imbedded in my head
Lies and tears and things unsaid
Remember, all thc nights of bitter pain

Everyone has come and gone
Casualties of a cause unknown
No matter what, it'll never be the same

Twisted thoughts hollow the bone
Leaving me again here all alone
Could you save me, or will you let me die

Give me back my naïve views
Happier never knowing the truth
Deserted in this desert of my dried up life

Detoured

Save your grace for those
For anyone who'll believe in it
As I believe in ghosts
The spectral apparitions
Reach intangible goals
Freeze the firewall and melt it down
At times you come so close
Not only gravity can drag you down
From all that you want
All that you need
And all of those things that you
Just can't see yeah
Plot a plan, a course
Prepare for accidents and second tries
Show them no remorse
Even when the hurt wells up inside
Apply temporary only
Cause there's no lengthy longevity
Find outlets, release
In persistence are tools to succeed
In all that you want
All that you need
And all of those things that you
Just can't see yeah
Whatever you see
You only believe
All that you want
All that you need
And all of those things that you
Just can't see yeah
Map a road for fun
Look it over in a year
Find all the detours
How they led you not there but here

Down The Drain

Take it off
Time has come for you and I
To get it on
Make a plan to spend the night
Dim the lights
Make our voyage through the dark
Lie down slow
Position yourself in an arc

All that I wanna do
Is slip slowly into you

Rip it off
Feel it coming back again
Pour it on
Pushing pound adrenalin
Turn me on
Take me to that special place
Have some fun
Sip and sample, lick and taste

All that I wanna do
Is slowly slip into you
Events too perfect to pass
A memory made to last

Tousled hair
Messy wild and loving it
Feel the flesh
Accumulating sins again
Take a breath
Preventing to avoid a stain
Wash away
The evidence down the drain

All that I wanna do
Is slip slowly into you
Events too perfect to pass
A memory made to last

Ever Clouded

Woke up today
And this cloud was overhead
Woke up today
And my thoughts were bleeding red
Woke up today
And the darkness filled my bed
Then I could see
All the evidence was clear
Overtaken me
And following everywhere
I am so alone **I am so alone** i.am.so.alone.
Woke up today
And the night it didn't end
Woke up today
And it all felt like pretend
Inside of me
Purged the burning like a sin
I am so alone **I am so alone** i.am.so.alone.
Woke up today
And the cloud was still above
Woke up today
And I knew that it would suck
Released a sigh
Cause I didn't give a fuck
I am so alone **I am so alone** i.am.so.alone.

Forgive Me

And for all the pain
That I've put you through
All of the shame
That I just can't undo
I can't believe that this is happening
Those words that were mean, you know I didn't mean
Forgive me, forgive me
Forgive me please
For all of the lies
That I told to you
All of the cries
A hurt that only grew
I see the wrong and I can see the mistakes
You need time and I will give as much as it takes
Forgive me, forgive me
Forgive me please
For all of the years
You wasted on me
All of the tears
Instead of being happy
Now I can't believe that this is happening
You were all I knew and now I don't know me
Forgive me, forgive me
Forgive me please
Forgive me, forgive me
Forgive me please

Fortified In Tenacity

Stand still
Eyes closed
Think of everything you know
Stand down
Back bend
Tired of this mess again
Slow down it's too fast
Want to make this last
You can't make me you
So please don't try to
Accept that I have flaws
We can defile them all
Raise brow
Lick lips
Feel how much caring can grip
Soft kiss
Hold hands
Drop some of those selfish demands

Slow down it's too fast
Want to make this last
You can't make me you
So please don't try to
Accept that I have flaws
We can defile them all
You have an image in your mind
But I can't be that guy
I have ways that's strange
But we'll adjust and rearrange

I HATE Your Ex-Girlfriend

My friend I've had some news to tell you for so long
Your previous love interest was a nightmare, I'm not wrong
You were never you with her believe me, glad she's gone
I hate your ex-girlfriend
She only brought you down
We never had a conversation
When she was around
I hate your ex-girlfriend
I knew it wouldn't last
If you ever see her again
Tell her to kiss my ass
Now I can see the old you resurface, and I'm glad
The pain she inflicted was obvious, it hurt bad
You seem so much healthier, and not so sad
I hate your ex-girlfriend
She used you like a toy
Cold and lifeless vampire
Sucked out all your joy
I hate your ex-girlfriend
Proud it didn't last
Her head is so fucking big
How'd she get it up her ass?
A captive to a monster you were, my good friend
Guess you can't see the lies and torture, until it ends
Finally she is away, I can say what I want to say
I hate your ex-girlfriend
And all she did to you
Every time you try to fuck her
You end up getting screwed
I hate your ex-girlfriend
She's such a little cunt
She is nothing special
Nothing anyone would want

Led By The Serpent

A boy's daydream turned gray
Frozen and worn, broke away
A want for something so bad
Succumb to the belly of the beast
        Let go of self-control
        All I had
                She, with claws and razor eyes
                Cut me up inside
                Left me with nothing
                A void I can't erase
A goddess she was, in my head
Signs pointing toward demon instead
Pride became shame and hatred
Love with jealousy destroyed it
        Handed her the key
        To Within me
                She, with claws and razor eyes
                Cut me up inside
                Left me with nothing
                A void I can't erase

                She, with claws and razor eyes
                Cut me up inside
                Left me with nothing
                A void I can't erase
                She took it all away
                Everything I had
                Left me with nothing
                A void and lost regrets

Macking on Pubescence (turning putrescent)

Left a message for you girl
Party tonight
Leave the stress behind at home
Just for a while
Throw your cares and all your clothes
Over there in a pile

Warm sin
Come on in
It's all pretend
So fantasize
And we'll bring it to life

Now get close enough to touch
Feel the skin
Before the next sun comes up
Let me in
Your parents will never know
Where all you've been

Warm sin
Come on in
It's all pretend
So fantasize
And we'll bring it to life

Want to kiss you everywhere
Yes down there
We'll share something beautiful
Without a care
Then we'll swear nothing happened
To the cops and the kids

Warm sin
Come on in
It's all pretend
So fantasize
And we'll bring it to life

Matador's Guts

Come like a ghost
In a flash, in a frame
In the corner of my cornea
Dizzy from the shock
Your beauty forms from a
A little spark
And in that same method
Spread your wings and exit
And leave me alone
Leave me here yelling to the dial tone

Go! Go!
Why did you have to go?
Go! Why did you go away?

Now like a flood
In a flash, in a sec
I become a nervous twitching wreck
Laying on the ground
So sure of instant death
Death of you, At least for me
And now, nothing can ever replace
The expression of your face

Go! You go!
Why'd you go away?
Go! Go! Why'd you have to
Go! Go!
Why'd you go away?

Come like a ghost
Leave like a flood
Was I, completely misunderstood
Or did I,
Never understand
What makes up
The science of woman
Women, women
And all the demands

Go! Go!
Why did you go away?
Why won't you stay?
You go!
Why'd you go away
From me, from me
Why couldn't you
Why couldn't you wait for me?

Come like a ghost, leave like a flood
Was I, was I misunderstood

Mislead Dreams

Awoke by the sound of knocking
Surprise visit you paid
Your eyes seem different than the last
Time, are you afraid?
You've come to reconcile and redeem
But the past I can't forgive
Only wanted love but that was
What you couldn't give
You stay away from me
Come what may
Turned out to be
Mislead dreams
I know you had your reasons
I know you needed time
I know your father went away
And he left you behind
But then the sting of rejection
Bestowed from you to me
Froze all contact and feelings
As now you finally see
You stay away from me
Come what may
Turned out to be
Mislead dreams
Go on and live the kind of life
You sacrificed to have
Know that you won't be forever
Stuck inside my head
You stay away from me
Come what may
Turned out to be
Mislead dreams
You stay away from me
Come what may
You and me
A mislead dream

Molt

What you say
And what you do
Floods with fear
On these aching limbs
Caustic lies
Made perfect fit
Your strings to tie
Molt me into shit

What you say, what you do
Plans of action include torturing, maiming
What you say, what you do
Broken and bruised, but I'm not giving in
Not giving in

What you say
And what you do
I'm just a game
That you play for fun
And I don't want
To end up alone
So store it up
I'll spill out someday

What you say, what you do
Plans of action include torturing, maiming
What you say, what you do
Broken and bruised, but I'm not giving in
Not giving in

It's what you say
And it's what you do
I had some hope
Couldn't see it through
It's all a joke
A silly storybook
All that I gave
Plus all you took and took

What you say, what you do
Plans of action include torturing, maiming
What you say, what you do
Broken and bruised, but I'm not giving in
Not giving in

Nothing Lasts When You're Young And Dumb

Saw your ex-girlfriend today
She didn't have too much to say
She looked the same, she hadn't changed
Except her hair and her last name
What happened to you?
What happened to you two?
All she could say was…
We were young, we were dumb
Didn't know what was to come
We loved quick, we lived fast
Didn't know it wouldn't last
But nothing lasts
Saw your ex-girlfriend today
Pretty page of your yesterday
Over time it grew estrange
So you threw it all away
What happened to you?
What happened to you two?
All she could say was…
We were young, we were dumb
Didn't know what was to come
We loved quick, we lived fast
Didn't know it wouldn't last
But nothing lasts
Nothing lasts
Nothing's the same
Everything is nothing
Nothing's everything
Saw your ex-girlfriend today
She said for me to tell you "hey"
As she walked the other way
I thought of all those angstful days
What happened to you?
What happened to you two?
All she could say was…
We were young, we were dumb
Didn't know what was to come
We loved quick, we lived fast
Didn't know it wouldn't last
But nothing lasts

Proven Disbelief

Keep your cool
Keep your senses
Throw yourself into psychosomatic strife
Make the worst mistake of my entire life
I just wanted you
But you never wanted me
You had to go and prove
All my disbelief
I tried make you laugh
But you only wanna cry
You had to show me love
Was a man made lie
A lie
A lie you hide
You hide
Plan your day plot a perfect course
Events will only change from bad to worse
Build up walls
For your defenses
Drown yourself in your synthetic bliss
There's nothing left for you to ever miss
I just wanted you
But you never wanted me
You had to go and prove
All my disbelief
I tried make you laugh
But you only wanna cry
You had to show me love
Was a man made lie
Lies
A disguise
Disguise
Wrap yourself in a disgusting sight
Only happy with a reason to fight
I just wanted you
But you never wanted me
You had to go and prove
All my disbelief
I tried make you laugh
But you only wanna cry
You had to show me love
Was a man made lie

Reanimate

Breaths come hard tonight
Wondering if you're alright
Death stopped by tonight
Told me to let go of the old life
But how can I forget
Something so permanent
Can we find faith in the stars above?
Can we reanimate this love?
Can we get back once it's gone?
Can we regenerate this bond?
Simple tasks today
Seem so complex to me
Try to make a sound
But the silence drowns me out
And how can I forget
Something significant
Can we find faith in the stars above?
Can we reanimate this love?
Can we get back once it's gone?
Can we regenerate this bond?
The price of freedom
A stable kingdom
The price of failure
To be without her
Can we find faith in the stars above?
Can we reanimate this love?
Can we get back once it's gone?
Can we regenerate this bond?

Redemption & Retribution

Gather around all mighty ones
Gaze upon the fool
Who twisted all the elders taught
Rewrote all the rules
He is held in captive now
Tortured for his crimes
Sentence will not be lifted
At the cost of any price

Throw the words, throw the stones
Taste the blood of those done wrong
Get a punch in, make a contribution
These high judges yield not a chance
Of retribution

Fortune favors no one here
In this freedom land
Everyone is a prisoner
By everybody else
Steal a key and then slip away
To find your beloved home
Even if you see the light of day
Your soul they'll forever own

Throw the words, throw the stones
Taste the blood of those done wrong
Get a punch in, make a contribution
These high judges yield not a chance
Of a redemption

If I ever forgive myself
Will anyone else?

The secret to the wisdom here
Is never finding out
Abandon curiosity
For it won't save you now
Every time you turn around
The knife is in your back
Everyone has a friendly face
Clinched ready for attack

Throw the words, throw the stones
Taste the blood of those done wrong
Get a punch in, make a contribution
These high judges yield not a chance
Of retribution
…Of a redemption

Skinner Box

Spectral riggers drip dry
A calico view
Seen by these eyes
Grinding bones and neon tones
Should've had the sense
To sense being alone
But now I am conditioned
I make no real decision
And you think you know me
Got old without the wisdom
Tell me what to do
I'll do it for you
I can be well trained
To perform in any way
A suburban fairy tale
Adds a flavoring
To what is stale
And though these bars invisible
It keeps me restrained
It keeps you amused
But now I am conditioned
I make no real decision
You think you can test me
But will I fail your prediction
Tell me what to do
I'll do it for you
I can be well trained
To perform in any way
And now I am conditioned
I make no real decision
Tell me what to do
I'll do it for you
I can be well trained
To perform in any way

StillBirth

Peek in
Dive down
Inject the venom
Into your veins
Sleepwalk
All day
On the change
You can't stay sane

And now the luster of
The goal we set to seek
Has ceased to shine on
The duration peak

And you pain
Your strain is great
Your pain pains me

Give up
Reset
Erase the ghost
Of forgotten tears
Empty
Trophies
Reject the duties
Go check the mirrors

And now the luster of
The goal we set to seek
Has ceased to shine on
The duration peak

And you pain
Your strain is great
Your pain pains me

Stillbirth
Still life
Afterbirth, After life
Whatever
You do or say
You'll waste your time
Waste your time away

And now the luster of
The goal we set to seek
Has ceased to shine on
The duration peak

And you pain
Your strain is great
Your pain pains me

To Carry On

Vengeance is the god, virtue is so odd
When all I really wanted was peace
Born an infamous son, in the valley of the gun
These urges raised never to cease
Victim of a crowd, outspoken by the loud
Abandoned with a false sense of dreams
Burdened by all the wrong, yet I seem to carry on
With the embracing of the media machines

Go…
Death, in life
Helpless, hopeless, scum
Dead, inside
Feel nothing for no one
Can't carry this weight of hardship
It breaks the spine in me
You'll never understand why
I can't let things be

Love it was the prize, the glisten in your eyes
But in the end was it all just a lie
A goal to achieve, to fill an empty need
But doesn't stop the hollowing inside
Tomorrow's not insured, I'm still not assured
That this cycle has a course yet to run
Broken up and broken down, crawling on the dirty ground
Will I survive all this damage done?

~ chorus ~

Life merely is a game, a trophy show of shame
Place your bets and watch the evil triumph
On a mission here to kill, any opposition's will
Advance to make the whole system corrupt
Surrounded by the plague, spreading out in every way
Inflicting in the hordes of herds of men
This life I would delete, start again clean slate
Yet the agony, hypocrisy won't end

~ chorus ~ x2

Toddling Follicles
(missing page in the book of psalms)

Make me cum, make me cry
Make me do those things that I
I swore against, fought against
Make me make a fierce repent
Make me go, make me stay
Make me turn my hope away
Away from me away from you
Away from all the shit you do
Transcend, Transcend any boundaries
Make me cum, make me cry
Make me do those things that I
I dream about, scream about
Let me let my demons out
Make me sad, make me smile
A trick to make this trip worthwhile
Make me burn, make me bleed
Leave me in my time of need
Transcend, Transcend any boundaries
I've been seeing you for so long
I forgot how to survive alone
Can't remember the old version of me
Can't remember how I used to be
Make me cum, make me cry
Make me feel the urge to die
Build me up, knock me down
Turn all of the guilt around
Make me shake, make me break
See how much that I can take
Make me fail, make me fall
Make me feel nothing at all
Transcend, Transcend any boundaries
(repeat second verse)
Transcend, Transcend any boundaries
I've been seeing you for so long
I forgot how to survive alone
Combining of two, losing of one
The integration has begun
Make me cum, make me cum
Make me cum, make me CUM…
Make me cum, make me cry…

Warranted Affection

Now these hands, once stout with stone, collapse and fall away
A diet wouldn't lose this weight that pulls inside of me
These death threats by the puppets, strangle all the air
I could tell your secrets aloud but I wouldn't dare
All alone, all alone, alone I am tonight
Staring at a broken fool I am sick of the sight
Now you say it isn't warranted
Can't breathe in these lungs
It's all the same I'm just a scapegoat
In the end it all just falls on me
So many times within my mind, a plot of your demise
Your plea of innocence rings false, I see it in your eyes
The gap the gaping hole won't close, wound cannot be stitched
Maybe you see the monster in me, in you I see a bitch
All alone, all alone, alone I await for you
I could describe but you still wouldn't have a fucking clue
Now you say it isn't warranted
Can't breathe in these lungs
It's all the same I'm just a scapegoat
In the end it all just falls on me
Here I sit beside myself to ponder all I lost
Every beginning forces endings, nothing gained without cost
Ripped from your side I will not die, I just float around
For better for worse I am not sure cause I'm always sinking down
All alone, all alone, alone I always am
I'd recite my feelings for you but you wouldn't give a damn
Now you say it isn't warranted
Can't breathe in these lungs
It's all the same I'm just a scapegoat
In the end watch me
As I bleed
As I bleed
As I bleed
As I bleed
As I bleed.

Words to a Stranger

Every time that I try to get with you, every time
You could not, for something's wrong
Did you plan this all along?
Every time I call to talk to you, never there
Still I wait in my room
Knowing you aren't getting through
Oh I don't want you …anymore

You won't attempt contact at all
So have your fun but when it's done
You'll be home, all alone, and I'll be gone
And when you find in retraction
All this passive inaction
Let it go, let it die, and don't you ever wonder why
Oh I don't want you…anymore

Oh I don't want you
You, and the things you do
Make me insane
Make me fall from grace
Fall from grace
I'm so out of place
When I fall from you
You, and the things you do…

So next time you are alone
And you need a friend
Don't call on me cause I'm not
About to wait in line
And you'll find over time
A good thing you left behind
Please try and understand
Cause I won't ever be your man
Oh I don't want you… anymore
No, I don't want you…anymore

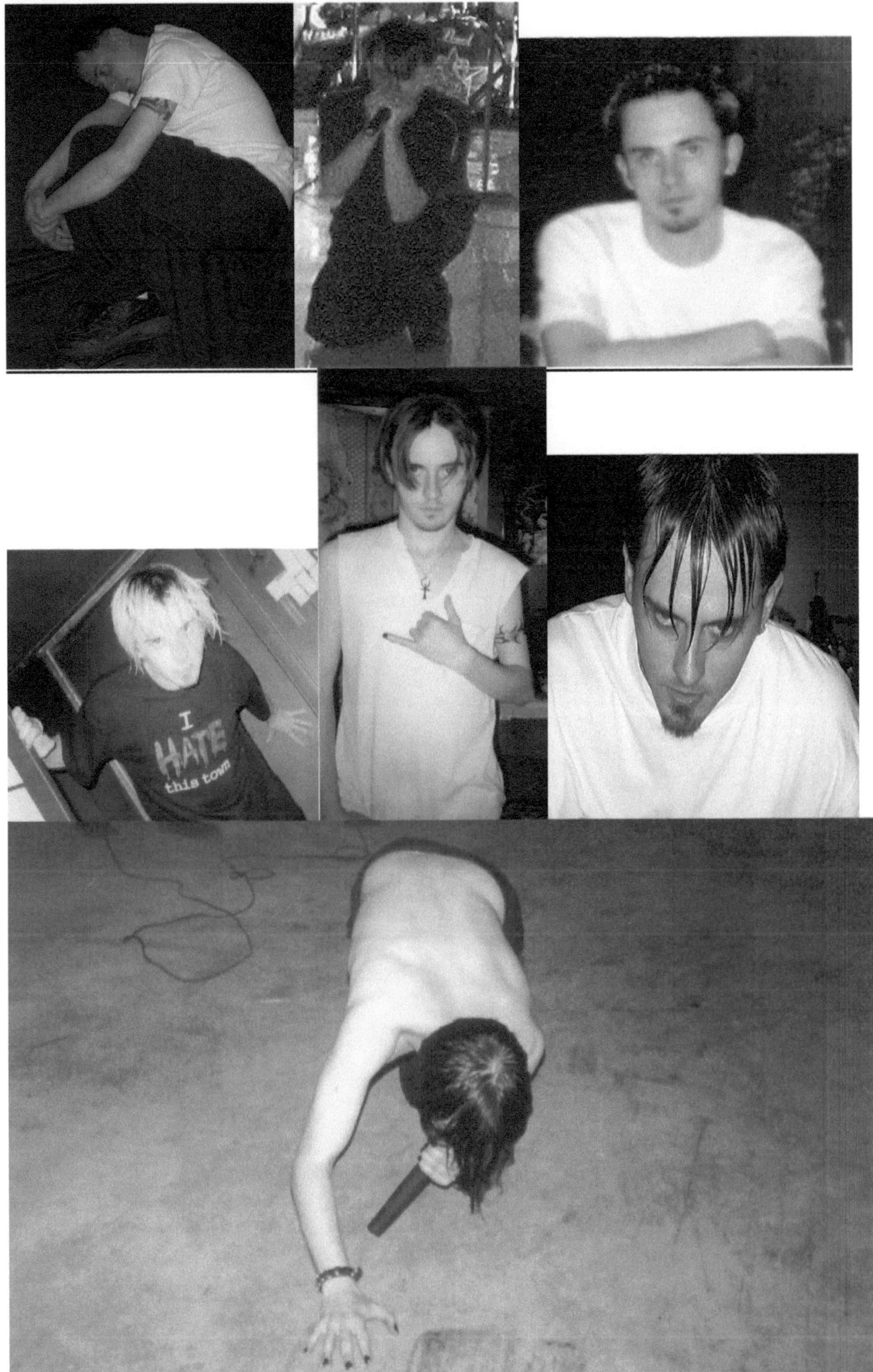
I
HATE
this town

www.ingramcontent.com/pod-product-compliance
Ingram Content Group UK Ltd.
Pitfield, Milton Keynes, MK11 3LW, UK
UKHW040601210726
13854UKWH00008B/1699

9 781105 540349